Blood, Sweat and Tears

Blood, Sweat and Tears

A RAJAM

NIYOGI
BOOKS

Published by
NIYOGI BOOKS
D-78, Okhla Industrial Area, Phase-I
New Delhi-110 020, INDIA
Tel: 91-11-26816301, 49327000
Fax: 91-11-26810483, 26813830
email: niyogibooks@gmail.com
website: www.niyogibooks.com

Editor: Gita Rajan
Design: Nabanita Das/Niyogi Books

ISBN: 978-93-81523-64-3
Publication: 2013

Printed at: Niyogi Offset Pvt. Ltd., New Delhi, India.

My late grandparents Ratnam and Leela
And to my great grandmother Saraswati

Prologue

She stood waiting in her pale pink leotard, in the tall-ceilinged audition room. The other two hopefuls stood on either side of her, the bright lights covering them all. They were inside the famous Moscow Star Ballet Theatre, the birthplace of so many stars. Where talented nobodys became somebodys. Three company directors sat at a rosewood table in front of them. Zaria could hear her breath as she consciously breathed in and breathed out. She felt sweat sluggishly trickle down her forehead, but didn't wipe it away. Was her perfume too heavy? Her brown hair was in a meticulously done bun with a silky hair-tie. Her feet sweated inside her new pointe shoes. She saw the stern looking grey haired former ballerina whispering furiously to the man next to her. Did they think her jetes weren't good enough? Restless, she shuffled her feet on the wooden floor. This was the moment. To her, life without ballet was like lifetime in prison. She could never accept that. Ever. She glanced at the round clock that hung above the directors' heads. When would they know? She pictured herself bowing regally, as dozens of roses were thrown at her feet. But to an observer, her face was inscrutable. She looked like she was just waiting for the bus. Her foundation felt so thick. The stony faced man shook his head. She moved her eyes to her right. The blonde had enthralled the directors. Zaria had felt such envy when she had seen her perfect pirouettes. The blonde would surely get the part. Zaria swallowed and then strained her ears to hear what the directors were saying. She prayed fervently, that they would like her. If she didn't make it, would she ever get a breakthrough, get a role in any ballet? All the years of hard work may never materialise. What if she never made it and just auditioned for years until she was forced to hang up her shoes wistfully? It would always remain a delusion.

The directors were certainly taking their time. They were conversing in hushed tones, in rapid Russian. Ten whole minutes passed. Then, suddenly, they stopped whispering and sat back in their tall chairs.

The stony faced man in the centre spoke first. He looked at the blonde girl with interest.

"You were really very good. Perfect twirls," the man said to her, nodding.

Zaria watched the blonde smirk and felt the dread inside her. No, no, no! She had lost it. So close….

Chapter 1

Irina and Zaria were in Moscow settling into the cramped hundred and fifty square foot apartment in the northern part of the city that Irina's parents lived in. The flat was very modestly furnished with walls of grey-blue paint, peeling in a few corners. A wooden floor in dark brown stood underneath the whole space which had just one bedroom and a tiny kitchen. Save for an old painting that hung on the wall, the décor was quite bare. A heater that thankfully worked all right stuck to the wall opposite the painting. A small, round dining table stood just outside the kitchen and a few chairs stood on the other end of the room, which served as a space for visitors.

Outside, the cold was so menacing, so extreme in the midst of the cruellest of winters. The temperatures were dipping lower and the ice covered everything from the trees to the sidewalks to rooftops to children's bicycles that had been left outside for a minute. The snow didn't listen to anyone's protests, didn't let anyone breathe. It laughed as the poor shivered and begged for mercy beneath blankets that were never thick enough. Irina felt throttled by it, the Russian winter she was experiencing after over a decade. The cold attacked her from everywhere, making her body feel frozen and trapped, making her heart more miserable than it already was. She was a widow in just her mid-thirties.

"You must pull yourself together," her father said, his arm around her as she cried. His face was caring, yet his tone was firm.

Irina nodded slowly as she wiped her cheeks that were streaked with fresh tears. She knew she needed her parents' moral support if she had to raise her child alone.

"This is such a shock for all of us, my child. But you must be strong…for Zaria," her mother said, looking towards the bedroom where Zaria was sleeping.

She took her daughter's hands in her own. Her grip was solid but there was an evident tightness in it. Irina could hear the message in them, the one saying that she couldn't fall apart. She had to go on. Even if she wanted to die.

The inner battles had to be fought, but she was unable to find the strength required of her. She felt like a doe thrown out amidst a snowstorm. Her mind was so fragile, so inept to deal with the severe trauma. She had never faced such adversity before. Her childhood years had not prepared her for it. Her married life had been just wonderful. And now it was gone.

"What can I do? I can't…" Irina sputtered.

In less than a minute she was crying again, unable to stop even when her head ached.

"I have to bring her up. But how can I support her?" she whispered. Her eyes were red, the pupils bloodshot to the core. An hour later fatigue overwhelmed her and she passed out with her head on the table.

In the days that followed, she was left to try and grope her way through the dark rocks every day, trying not to fall. Preethi, her sister-in-law, e-mailed her from India asking how she was coping, but Irina didn't want to tell her about her heartache. Who would want to listen to a grown up whining about her life? What qualifications did she have? No vocational skills, no professional qualifications. Not even a college degree. She needed a plan to stay afloat, to make ends meet. But what was she to do ? She felt she needed psychiatric counselling, but knew she couldn't think about herself. She had a child to raise. Zaria had to come first, and she had to find a job to support her. But where?

At first, she wanted to go back to teaching ballet. Her old friend Olga ran a well-known ballet school and she said Irina could definitely teach there once classes commenced again in a few months. She was a close friend of Irina's and was genuinely concerned. They had no classes during the winter break and so Irina had to look elsewhere for immediate money. Trying to get the required paperwork done since they had immigrated was the immediate issue. Zaria was already a Russian citizen thanks to her mother, but that wasn't making the process easier. They had a roof over their heads at least, which many did not even have.

In five days, Irina got herself a job as a waitress in a small restaurant. She was expected to work more than seven hours a day and was away for most of the evening, trying to scrimp and save to put food on Zaria's plate. Her father Mikhail had retired from teaching and so had her mother Galya due to her bad knee condition. Whatever money they had saved had been carefully set aside in the bank for their old age. So they were unable to help their daughter financially despite wanting to. Irina wasn't just alone now, she had a child to care for, a child she loved more than anything else in the world. But her mind was plagued by doubts. What if she couldn't give Zaria the childhood she had always wanted to give her? What if she could never find the time to be the kind of mother she wanted to be? She cried to her parents, saying that she felt broken into pieces and didn't know how to pick them up and put them together. At night, she spent many hours crying. She could barely sleep for the first few weeks without Rajiv next to her. Even during the day, she cried many times when she was alone, the sheer frustration of her existence making her feel insignificant in the brutality of the world. She went to a synagogue every week, praying that God would give her the strength to go on with life. She wished the agony would fade slowly, but it did not even seem to lessen.

Moscow wasn't the same city which she had left to get married. Since the fall of the Soviet Union in 1991, the USSR no longer existed. Irina had no time to even notice the changes. Being a single mother couldn't have been harder than at that time. Moscow was presently in a phase where everything was extremely expensive. Prices had shot up and she had to buy food from discount shops, clothes from street markets and a few woollen coats to make sure she and Zaria didn't die of pneumonia. Olga asked her why she couldn't simply remarry, to make things easier.

"No way. I don't want a drunken Russian husband," Irina would reiterate firmly. Remarrying was completely out of the question. She was still trying to recover from the rude shock of losing her husband. Perhaps the phase of torture she had to deal with was something that she had had to learn from. With her faith and prayers, Irina accepted her fate. She took on some odd jobs, which was the only thing she was qualified for. Every morning, she waited tables at a Russian restaurant for over six hours. And at night she was a barmaid. She had done the same job when younger when she wasn't dancing in the summers, to earn pocket money. Many times she felt the strain of pushing herself. Suddenly, the chaos of hell would choke her and make her gasp for breath. At times she found herself sweating profusely and getting breathless, her heartbeats quickening, wondering if she would get through the hellish phase. But there was no time to think about herself. She had to get her life together for her daughter.

The low profile bar she worked at night in was a small one, in the upstairs of a building which also had some cheap restaurants. The room where the bar was had just six tables—low, wooden ones with large chairs which were a contrast to the almost yellow white walls. Some pictures of scenes from Russian thriller movies were scattered around one wall. The floor was bare with no carpet laid on it for people's tired feet. High stools with black cushions stood around where Irina mixed the drinks, where she sweated and toiled in her bartender's uniform. Two dozen high, tall shelves stocked with every kind of liquor rose behind her, speedily getting emptied out by drunkards. The mix of alcohol, cigarettes and mustiness made her feel out of place.

She glanced with apprehension at the crowd that filled the room. Most were working men and women who worked late and usually stopped by for a drink before heading home. The atmosphere was rowdy, scary for someone who wasn't from Moscow. Many faces littered the chairs—seedy faces, young ones, old ones; they were all bent on drowning their sorrows in bottles of alcohol.

Irina stood behind the counter, having just re-learnt everything about all the different kinds of vodka, beer, whisky and wine. The bottles felt so unfamiliar as she poured from them, trying to get impatient customers satisfied.

"Hurry up with our drinks you damn woman!" came a rough voice from the stools to her right.

The men who sat there looked like they could have been from the Mafia, but Irina didn't think about who she was serving. The group on the other side of the bar was making enough noise to give her a headache. She had just cut one of them off because he was too drunk, and had started acting funny. He had abused her for doing so. So much that she had moved away from the table fast. She could feel a lot of male eyes on her, as she mixed their drinks. Those eyes would roam over her as she served them and some would even ask her for sexual favours, their speech slurred with drunkenness. She hated it, hated the smell of liquor on their breath. She felt so out of place working there, but went on, knowing she had no other choice. The pay was good and that's what she had to hold on to.

She worked at the bar every night, late into the night. She kept telling herself that once the ballet classes at her old school restarted she could stop working at the scary place. Until then Irina forced herself to get used to her new hurried rhythm of life.

One night, when business happened to be unusually slow, she found her thoughts straying elsewhere. They pulled her to her past in India, to the city then called Madras. She felt so different, so at peace, as she remembered the love she had known there.

At first, she hadn't seen the young man staring at her. Indian men's stares were nothing new from what she had seen since her arrival. But this look was different. It wasn't remotely like the cheap stares she had gotten when she walked on the street that seemed to undress her with their intensity. He just seemed to be admiring her from afar. When she chanced to meet his eye, he had smiled.

She and a fellow ballerina, along with two renowned Bharatanatyam dancers, had just performed a fusion of ballet and Bharatanatyam to begin the evening meant to commemorate Indo-Russian relations. They had performed at the Taj Coromandel Hotel ballroom to a select audience from the city, including diplomats from the local Russian and other Consulates.

The arts pages in the city papers carried several articles about the visiting ballerinas. The show generated a lot of excitement as the famous European dance form had not been performed in Madras for well over ten years. After all, it was when Rukmini Devi Arundale, the legendary Indian dancer, had met Anna Pavlova on a ship and Pavlova had told her to start her own dance school that the famous Kalakshetra was born. That was a fitting prelude to the moment when the two dance forms were being blended.

The curtains rose, revealing the visiting ballerinas in their light blue and pearly white tutus. Four of them were on the stage–Irina, Elena, Sudhalakshmi and Urmila. They performed a shortened version of the famous *Swan Lake*. The Indian dancers were playing the swans, dressed in traditional white and gold costumes. They wore gold-plated jewellery and the fan in front of their costume spilled out in a beautifully patterned gold design. The music flowed from western classical sound to Indian beats between scenes. India's cultural hub, Madras, had responded tremendously. Most of the chairs in the hall were filled. When, in the final act, the two lovers were forced to throw themselves into the lake, the audience was quiet, empathising with the sad ending. All the dancers held hands and bowed to very generous applause.

In the audience was Rajiv Krishnan, whose company was one of the main sponsors of the event. He was the admirer whose stares and smile had drawn Irina's attention. Rajiv's parents desperately wanted him to settle down as he was nearly twenty-eight. The girl they had their eye on was Raima, the daughter of their dear friends.

"Raima has grown up to be such a lovely young lady. And ambitious too. She wants to be a designer," Rajiv's mother Jaya had said to him one day.

Rajiv had met her in his parents' living room on their request three weeks ago. She was a few years out of college and, from her overly flirtatious manner, clearly as keen as his parents on the match. Rajiv had felt a little irritated with the way his parents seemed to take his acceptance for granted. He thought she was pretty, but had a conceited and self-centred air about her.

He met with Raima a few times to please his parents but soon knew he had to state the truth.

He spoke his mind firmly to drive home the point. "Amma, Appa, I'm not sure how to say this, but I don't think Raima will work out."

The shower of hot, angry words rained down on him, just as he had expected.

"Rajiv, how can you say that? What do you mean?" his mother Jaya said, with a tone of evident anger in her stern voice.

"What rubbish! She is as lovely as her mother before her," said his father Sanjay, sounding bewildered.

Rajiv had been prepared for the arguments and they poured forth with increasing stridency. But he stood his ground and his parents had no choice but to give up.

All the dancers stayed for the champagne and snacks following the show. Rajiv found that he couldn't quite take his eyes off one gorgeous young Russian ballerina; Irina wore a knee-length white skirt and a pearly white satin top which showed off her graceful shoulders and neck. Her blonde hair was swept into a bun. Rajiv thought she looked angelic. That was the first word that came to his mind amidst all the shades of white she wore. On her neck was a string of pearls, the drops as delicate as her features—the perfect chin, the sculpted small nose and the soft green eyes that he couldn't help staring at. From the first time he had set eyes on her, something had stirred deep within him. The desire, the longing to know more about the young Russian beauty. It was an instant crush.

Rajiv walked up to Irina and Elena as they chatted with some of the guests.

"Once again, all of us sponsors want to thank you for a splendid show," he said, smiling and shaking their hands.

"Thank you for your sponsorship support," Irina replied with a shy smile.

Her first thought was that he was soft-spoken and charming. He asked how they liked the city and what their impression of his hometown was.

"We are already at home here thanks to the warm, hospitable people," Elena said.

"We loved seeing the temples and watching some Indian dancers perform," Irina added.

She spoke about how interesting the culture and food in India were and added that she had learnt a few Tamil phrases already.

Rajiv and Irina kept talking for nearly an hour without paying any attention to the time. Neither grew tired of the other's company. At the end of the evening, Rajiv hesitantly asked her for her phone number. Irina was surprised but pleased as well. Why not? She was single and he seemed like a nice man. She wrote down the phone number of Urmila's house where she was staying. He asked if she would have dinner with him on Saturday and she accepted his invitation.

Chapter 2

On their first date Rajiv took Irina to dinner at the Adyar Gate Hotel, which was one of the few starred hotels in the city. The luxuriousness of the place made Irina feel he was spending too much, but she remained silent. They were seated at a table for two near the window and attracted a lot of attention from some other diners who knew Rajiv. But he was unaware of them and focussed entirely on Irina. He was avidly interested in knowing everything about her and she gave him all the details.

She was born in Moscow to Jewish parents, Galya and Mikhail Medievsky. Her mother was a professor of English, teaching Russian students at a local language centre in Moscow. Her father was a professor of Economics at a high school and had taught at University earlier.

"Wow. Both parents are professors? Did they place a lot of emphasis on education?" Rajiv asked, looking impressed.

"Well, yes, they ensured that I worked well at school. But they also encouraged my interest in ballet," Irina said.

Initially she had been a bit hesitant to tell him about her parents because she had heard that he came from one of the wealthier families in the city. From what she had heard of India, the rich boy and poorer girl story was not the most popular.

"I went to a full-time ballet school from the age of thirteen and started dancing professionally from eighteen, when my training was done. Dancing was always my passion," she continued, opening up easily.

Rajiv smiled.

"I can see how much you love being a dancer. Tell me all about it. Where did you start learning?" he said, leaning forward.

She laughed.

"I didn't think you'd be interested in any of that," she said, with a shy smile.

"I'm interested in knowing everything about you…" he said, looking at her intensely. Irina blushed.

She ate small mouthfuls of the Caesar Salad she had ordered, munching on the lettuce slowly when she was too shy to speak. The soft, silky black dress that she wore clung to her.

"I started learning when I was only three at a ballet school not too far from home…" she started, her eyes turning nostalgic. Rajiv noticed the fondness in her recollections as she spoke. She went on as he nodded, urging her to continue. She told him everything about herself—her childhood, her excitement on buying her first ballet shoes, her schooldays and days at the ballet academy, her travels, her two not so serious relationships.

"As I was so focussed on ballet training and performing, where was the time?" she joked. He let her speak about whatever she wanted to and listened. He said he had a younger sister called Preethi. They were very close. She was doing some interior design work having graduated from college with a fine arts degree.

On Rajiv's request, Irina continued telling him her story.

Rajiv listened with interest as he ate his fried fish, and asked about the Bharatanatyam workshop she had attended.

"It was initially a little funny," Irina giggled. "At first, we were a little too dainty. I remember the time when the Bharatanatyam teacher kept telling us to bring our feet down on the floor harder and harder until Elena hurt her foot from slamming it down with too much force. It was hilarious." she said.

Rajiv listened patiently as she spoke of her travel experiences and about her long-standing desire to visit India. She was only twenty-three but had already performed with the famous Baranski Theatre in Moscow in many lead roles. Rajiv was very impressed and he told her so.

"So young, so lovely and so accomplished," were the words he used. Irina's shyness faded slowly, and by the end of their date she felt as though she had known Rajiv for a very long time.

Within hours of their dinner, many people in town had inevitably heard about their date. One of the people at the nearby table at the restaurant, whom Rajiv had tried hard to avoid speaking to, had started the gossip flowing. Soon the people at the Madras Club, where Rajiv often went, were discussing it in earnest, as the story spread from one to the other.

"That Russian ballerina? So soon after Raima didn't work out? Jaya will surely be furious. She is so traditional."

On the professional front, Irina's dance career was on the upswing and her profile was highly documented in the media. She gave an interview to the English newspaper *The Hindu* and talked about her lead roles with the Baranski ballet group in Moscow. The Arts Section there and a local Tamil magazine carried interviews with her and Elena. Irina spoke about the roles she had danced, the various countries she had toured to and her love of Russian culture. The articles praised her as one of the biggest stars in Russian ballet.

Irina began to feel a strong attraction to Rajiv and more dates followed. One was to a south Indian restaurant. Then they dined at the Golden Dragon Chinese restaurant at another hotel. The posh dinner dates were great but Irina told him frankly that he didn't have to take her to expensive places. She wanted to see Indian culture and know more about it.

He laughed. "All right then," he said.

He took her to see the Rock Temple sculptures in Mahabalipuram. Irina loved them. She also enjoyed seeing the Chola bronzes at the Madras museum. The city in those years had practically no malls, a few cinema theatres and fewer restaurants. But Rajiv took her to every place he could think of. He took her to a store that sold salwar kameez and she exclaimed at the range of colourful designs. They browsed for costume jewellery in Mylapore. Irina really enjoyed simple things like walking with Rajiv on the Besant Nagar beach. She ventured to taste the raw mangoes and chilli powder sold by vendors and thoroughly enjoyed the delicious roasted corn and *sundal*.

The buds of their romance started to blossom as the summer wore down. The courtship wasn't cooling down though. Irina's Indian friends told her that Rajiv had very nearly been engaged. He, however, assured her that he was genuinely attracted to her. He had told his friends that it was love at first sight. Irina was by nature demure and quiet. Since her schooldays she had been extremely shy with boys, despite her good looks.

She thought it was very sweet of Rajiv to show her around the city so assiduously. Meanwhile, tongues in the city were wagging furiously about the Indian man and his Russian girlfriend. News of their dates soon practically became the staple diet of the socialite circle of Madras.

"Rajiv Krishnan is falling for a foreign woman?" "Yes, she is beautiful…but his parents will be furious. They are so conservative."

Irina was not trying to hook Rajiv for his money. She wasn't that kind of a girl. But she courted the secret envy of many other girls who had harboured hopes of being Mrs Rajiv Krishnan. He was one of the most eligible bachelors in town given his family name, money, good looks and personality. His parents were amongst the most respected and wealthy people in Madras. They had a very successful business of dealing in automobiles. Jaya and Sanjay Krishnan were very traditional-minded like many of their generation in eighties-India.

Rajiv found himself falling in love faster than he thought possible. Each time he met Irina, his feelings grew stronger.

"I'm ever so fascinated by your country and its culture. People are so hospitable and welcoming," Irina told him.

She had felt a connection with India the moment she set foot in the country. She felt herself falling in love with the people and its calm beauty. This was besides the love that started to grow within her for Rajiv himself. She loved that he was a gentleman, unlike many other men she had met who only lusted after her body. She had never met someone like him before, someone who was so genuinely interested in just getting to know her. He never attempted to get too physical. They went to Nageshwara Park and sat around, talking for hours. She told him of her love for books, her best friends at home and her favourite songs. He told her how he had been an avid batsman in cricket in his school and college days and how he still loved to watch live matches at the Chepauk Stadium. She listened as he spoke of his love for cars and his favourite Hollywood films. They shared an easy camaraderie.

Rajiv was also very romantic. He sent Irina a bouquet of red roses after they had gone on their third date. He bought her gifts—a gorgeous silver necklace, a silk sari from the Nalli Silk Store. She knew she was falling for his charms very fast. At the end of the month, they were both in love. Neither said it aloud, but both knew it.

When it was time for Irina to go back to Russia, Rajiv realised he was very much in love, as madly in love as a man could be. Irina was very sad that she had to leave.

"I hope we'll keep in touch. Maybe you can write to me sometimes?" she asked, looking at him sadly. Rajiv smiled.

"Of course I'll write to you. I wish you didn't have to leave," he said, his eyes showing his frustration. He gave her a warm hug, and she hugged him back for a long moment before she said goodbye and left to pack. She had given Rajiv her phone number in Moscow but since they were both going to be busy travelling on work, she didn't expect to be able to talk to him.

Irina said goodbye to all her Indian friends from the dance school. She told them to get in touch with her if they ever happened to visit Russia.

Before she knew it, Irina was on the flight back home. As the plane took off, she wistfully thought of her eventful time in India and the romance that seemed to have ended too soon. She remembered the date when Rajiv had taken her to watch a Bollywood movie at the Safire Theatre complex. She thought the melodies and song and dance sequences were spectacular. She giggled throughout the songs where the actors ran around trees. She remembered their first kiss. In her heart, she knew that she would remember her three month stay in India as one of the most extraordinary places she had visited in all her travels.

She was sad thinking of the fact that she might never see Rajiv again. Perhaps he would write. Perhaps…

Chapter 3

A week later, on a Sunday morning, Irina heard the sound of the doorbell ringing. It was not even seven and she was still in her bathrobe. She yawned, ran a hand through her hair and walked to the door. When she opened it, she nearly fainted when she saw the person standing outside.

"Oh my God! Rajiv!" she gasped, almost stumbling in surprise.

Her cheeks flushed pink as she drew her woollen robe tighter around herself. The thought flashed across that she must be looking very sloppy with her tousled hair and sleep bedraggled appearance. She blushed deeper at the coincidence of his appearing just when she had been thinking about him, as though she had rubbed a magic lamp.

Rajiv was wearing a checked blue shirt and jeans.

"Hello Irina," he said, extending his right hand from behind his back. He held out a bouquet of long-stemmed red roses.

"Oh, what beautiful flowers! Thank you," Irina said, taking the flowers and inhaling their sweet scent. Neither of them spoke for a few seconds, an awkwardness hanging between them. Irina wanted to hug him and tell him that she had missed him terribly but instead managed to compose herself and say, "So what brings you to Moscow?"

Rajiv mumbled something about having to pass through Europe on a business trip to America and deciding to drop by and say hello. She had to smile at his explanation.

"So, um, would you like to come in and meet my parents?" she asked hesitantly. She wasn't sure how to explain to them why Rajiv had landed on their doorstep unannounced.

"Of course. That will be lovely," Rajiv said.

Irina ushered him into the small apartment and led him into the small sitting area on the left. Her father seemed to have gone out. She walked up to where her mother Galya sat, reading a book. On seeing the visitor, Galya looked up and adjusted her glasses.

"Oh, who is this? One of your Indian friends?" she asked, a note of interest in her voice. She was in her mid-forties and plump, with curly blonde hair.

"Mama, this is Rajiv. We became friends in Madras. I told you, remember?" Irina said, gesturing towards Rajiv. She was sure that her mother had sensed her feelings for Rajiv when she had spoken about him to her over the last week. Galya had that uncanny mother's instinct when it came to her only child.

Rajiv walked up to Galya and shook her hand.

"Nice to meet you Mrs Medievsky," he said politely.

Galya smiled and said, "Irina has told us about you. You have become a good friend of hers from what I hear."

She flashed a knowing look at Irina. Rajiv glanced at Irina and she blushed for the third time since he had arrived.

"So, Rajiv, I am an Indophile. I've read so much about your country's magnificent culture. Irina also told me a lot about her amazing trip," Galya said.

"I can tell you more about India if you would like," Rajiv said.

"That would be lovely, my dear. Sit down," Galya said, gesturing to the chair on her left. She put down the book she was reading on the small, wooden table beside her and started asking Rajiv about India.

Soon they were deep in conversation. Galya asked Rajiv everything about India and he asked her about her years of teaching English. He certainly knows how to charm people, Irina thought. He asked Galya a lot about Irina and she told him everything he wanted to know. Galya mentioned that she was a fan of the legendary Indian actor Raj Kapoor who started a craze amongst Russians in the fifties. Rajiv found her India obsession flattering and remarked on her substantial knowledge of his country. They seem to have hit it off, Irina thought, inwardly glad.

Galya then led Rajiv to the corner of the room and showed him all the photographs that stood on a mahogany mantelpiece.

"Here is Irina singing in her fifth grade school play," she said, pointing to a framed picture of a young blonde girl in a blue frock standing with her hands in front of her. Rajiv remarked that the same quiet grace that Irina had now was evident in the poised way that she held herself at a young age. Galya then opened a photo album and showed him pictures from Irina's performances and newspaper cuttings of her shows that she had saved. Rajiv looked at them with great interest and was very impressed. They both then sat down flipping through and discussing all the pictures from Irina's childhood, teenage years and college days. Irina excused herself to take a shower.

She showered and dressed quickly but stayed in her room, giving herself a moment to think. Rajiv seemed very earnest in wanting to know more about her. Was he in love with her? He hadn't actually said so, though she had heard he had told his friends that he was. She knew deep down that she was in love with him too.

She leaned against the bookcase on her left, took a deep breath, and let it all out. Why had he come to visit her so suddenly and from such a distance?

She watched Rajiv and her mother talking and jokingly said, “Hey I don’t think you both remember my existence.”

They looked in her direction and laughed.

“Hey mama, since Rajiv is here only for a short while I thought I would take him to the park for a bit,” Irina said, glancing at Rajiv hesitantly.

Galya smiled at him and asked, “Does he have the time?”

“Um, yes I do. I would like to, um, be shown around,” Rajiv said. He sounded unsure, which was unusual. Irina noticed that he was fidgeting with his hands.

Just then the front door opened and Irina’s father Mikhail walked in. He was tall and sturdily built, with dark brown hair that was thinning in the front. He had a kind face. Rajiv stood up on seeing him. Mikhail noticed the stranger and walked up to him.

“And who is this young man?” he asked as he shook Rajiv’s hand.

“I’m Rajiv, sir.” Rajiv introduced himself. “Mrs Medievsky was just showing me some photo albums.”

“Nice to meet you Rajiv. We heard you are a businessman, right?” Mikhail asked.

“That’s right, I am,” Rajiv said. Mikhail chatted with him for a minute before he went to the kitchen to fix himself a drink. Rajiv followed him and soon they were both chatting away about cars over a glass of vodka. Mikhail then told Rajiv about his car, a Lada, and how it wasn’t working.

“Why don’t we both go outside and take a look? I know something about fixing these things,” Rajiv offered.

“That would be great. Right this way,” Mikhail said. He gave Rajiv a friendly pat on the back and they both walked outside to the garage.

Irina walked to the window and looked at them as they stood near the pale indigo car. Her father had bought it from someone who sold used cars and he was very attached to it. Rajiv was soon underneath the hood.

Twenty minutes later, they both walked back into the house. Irina was sitting in a chair next to her mother and glanced up.

"What a boy! He fixed the thing like an expert. I don't have to worry about a repair job now," Mikhail announced, beaming.

Rajiv's hair had some grease spots on it. Irina's heart lurched. She knew how much father loved his Lada and the fact that Rajiv managed to fix it must have raised his esteem in her father's eyes. He seemed to be bonding with her parents really well.

Irina was sure Rajiv hadn't come to Moscow on work or because his "flight was delayed"—the excuse he offered as to why he was still there the next day. She felt rather flattered at the possibility that he had come all the way just to spend time with her. Her hopes had soared on seeing him again. Perhaps the things that they had left unsaid would burst forth on their own volition.

"Friendship Park," Irina announced, as they walked into the park on the northern outskirts of Moscow after a bus ride.

"I go for walks here sometimes," she added, "whenever I need space to think."

Rajiv and Irina walked across the green grass of the lawns, the cool breeze from the evening blowing over the few people scattered around the park. Their voices were very faint, barely stirring the quiet space. The sun shone down through the clouds, its rays spreading its warmth through the chilly air. The freshness of nature enveloped Irina. They strolled across the lawn to a corner that was almost deserted. A light drizzle sprung up, the drops of rain falling lightly, like a thin veil and slowly getting heavier. Some of the people got up and started going away but Irina and Rajiv stayed on the grass, not minding getting wet. They didn't talk much as they walked.

Suddenly, Rajiv stopped in front of her and to her astonishment, dropped down on one knee.

Oh my God…Is he? Irina's heart raced. Rajiv reached into his pocket and pulled out a ring with a small diamond studded on it. In that instant Irina realised that she wanted exactly the same thing. She said yes. It felt completely right even though she hadn't known him for more than a few months.

They shared a long kiss and started walking back, hand in hand. The raindrops fell faster, soaking Irina's hair. This made her laugh!

When they got home and broke the news, Irina's parents were delighted. They liked Rajiv already for the good impression he had made in their short meeting and respected their daughter's choice.

She would be part of a new life now. She would be in India, the mysterious country of culture that she was dying to know more about. She couldn't have found a more perfect man, she thought contentedly. He was her soul mate. The thought of leaving her ballet career midway, when she was at the peak, made her uneasy and a trifle unhappy, but fate did take strange turns. She wanted to blend into society in India and be accepted, especially by the two that she wanted to accept her the most—Rajiv's parents.

Rajiv's parents were as furious as could be imagined. They didn't want their son to marry a foreign woman. Jaya said she would never allow Rajiv to step into their house if he went ahead with the wedding. Rajiv's parents tried everything they could to change his mind, but to no avail. Irina was terribly upset about them not liking her. She cried. She felt like a misfit piece in the puzzle, the ugly duckling. Being shunned tore her up inside like a stab wound. She was lovely but not Indian, they had told him. The essential ingredient. The one thing even a genie couldn't make her.

Rajiv did not have a lot of money of his own since his father was the head of the family business and he was controlling the reins, with Rajiv as his understudy. But Rajiv had saved enough from his salary to take care of the wedding expenses himself. Preethi ran around to take care of all the arrangements.

In the end, for appearances sake, his parents agreed to grace the marriage with their presence, though they made it clear to Rajiv that they had not yet endorsed his choice of life partner. The wedding was the most talked about on the social calendar that year in Madras. It was the hottest news in town, billed as the exotic marriage of the decade. Comparisons were made to the famous Roerich-Devika Rani nuptials in 1945. The ceremony was attended by guests from all over India and the cream of Madras society. Before Irina knew it, she and Rajiv were husband and wife.

Irina loved every minute of her married life. She blended well into the society circles and being Mrs Krishnan was far easier than she had feared. She was soon admired for her sweet nature, beauty and elegant way of dressing.

Irina missed ballet, but started teaching classes at the Russian Cultural Centre twice a week. She loved teaching the toddlers who came to the classes. She enjoyed her new slow paced life and loved the luxury of living in their new, four bedroom house in a quiet part of town. Preethi and she became as close as sisters and talked about everything under the sun, without reserve. Within a year, Irina felt as though she had been in Madras all her life.

Everyone said that Irina and Rajiv looked so much in love that it must have been destiny that brought them together.

Chapter 4

A year later, on a cool evening in September, Rajiv and Irina's daughter was brought into the world. Irina named her Zaria which meant sunrise. She gave her the middle name Maya after the Russian ballet legend Maya Plizetskaya whom she had idolised since a child.

Zaria was a cheerful child, playful and talkative, the undisputed apple of her parents' eye. Being an only child was perfect for the little girl who enjoyed all the attention showered on her by her grandparents who had no reservations whatsoever about accepting her, their first grandchild. They loved her for her brightness and liveliness. The toddler lived up to her name—sunrise.

She was a student of the Alpha School since kindergarten and thoroughly enjoyed her days there. She learnt Bharatanatyam with a group of children twice a week. But it was ballet that she loved the most. Her mother had started her on it from the time she was three, and she learnt it at the Russian Cultural Centre twice a week with a group of other kids her age.

Irina gave her daughter an extra ballet lesson at home once a week in their white-floored veranda. As she raised her leg on the barres installed along one wall and demonstrated a stretch, she saw that Zaria was not even looking.

"Stop running about and pay attention!" Irina said, half-angry, half-amused at her child's attempts to do a cartwheel. Zaria would practise cartwheels a lot. She would never sit still during her mother's personal lessons until the day her mother showed her a video of one of her shows.

Zaria was held mesmerised as she watched the ballerinas move, their limbs so agile, so fluid. For over an hour, her eyes were glued to the screen, barely blinking. She did not speak even once. When the tape finished, she turned to her mother.

"Wow, they can move like angels," she said, her voice suddenly quiet, her eyes sparkling with wonder.

She felt her mother's hand on her shoulder and knew she was touched to hear her words of genuine admiration.

The bundle of energy that her daughter was sometimes frustrated Irina, but charmed her more. She ensured that Zaria grew up speaking English, Tamil and Russian. Irina always spoke to her in Russian, wanting her to know the language of her maternal grandparents. Zaria only knew a few words of Hebrew, though her mother spoke the language fluently. Irina was more adamant that she spoke, read and wrote Russian well since it was a part of her homeland, a part of which she wanted Zaria to have. She was earnest that her daughter knew about her Russian side and heritage. She would read Zaria Russian folktales like "Masha and the Bear" and the "Snow Maiden." She also told her stories that she had read from Indian mythology—stories from the Ramayana, the Jatakas, Akbar and Birbal and the witty tales of Tenali Rama the court jester. Irina's in-laws grudgingly gave her credit for this.

Rajiv was both a caring father and a doting husband. He travelled often, but called home everyday if he was away for long. He pampered his wife and made sure she would want for nothing. Irina loved her life in the city of Madras, its low-key people and quiet beauty. Though she missed her homeland, she grew to love India more with each passing day.

Zaria's interest in her ballet lessons grew rapidly, much to her mother's joy. She was a quick learner and her teacher told Irina that she was the best in her grade at the ballet classes. When Zaria's dance school had performances Irina was usually the one in the front row, the proud mother who snapped pictures of her child on stage.

At school, in the fourth grade, Zaria thought it very funny when she heard that Ashwin, a boy in their class, had a crush on her. He was a skinny, curly haired boy whom she sometimes found staring at her in class. Tara and Gul, her two best friends, found this hilarious. They teased her about it, saying all the boys said that Ashwin had admitted to having a crush on Zaria, who he said was "the prettiest girl in class." Soon all the girls in class were teasing Zaria about it. Ashwin looked embarrassed if Zaria just said hello to him and hardly said a word to her.

The city of Madras, the quiet, culture-rich city had captivated Irina. Irina felt that fate had drawn her there where she was so blissful that she thought she could never be happier. Everything in her life seemed almost too perfect to be real. Rajiv and she were still so much in love. She should have known it was too good to last forever.

"Irina! Stop daydreaming!" a rough voice rang out, rudely interrupting her reverie and bringing Irina back to the present with a thud. It was the owner of the bar. She realised that a customer had been trying to get her attention and quickly muttered her apologies to him. As she poured his drink, she lost her grip on the bottle and it shattered on the floor. She stumbled as she tried to pick up the broken pieces, the glass cutting her palms. The owner was impatient with her slowness and shouted at her. Irina cried on the way home.

She needed time for her heart to heal, for the deep wounds to close. More than once she imagined seeing Rajiv's face in the visage of the strangers who came into the restaurant. She saw his face in men sitting at the table by the window, sipping their coffees. His shadow would cross her when she walked on the streets and looked at people's faces. But it was never him. He was gone.

Irina was scared of losing her way but found that her prayers gave her strength to carry on. She enrolled Zaria in a free public school not very far from their neighbourhood. Zaria settled in quickly. She could already read and write Russian thanks to Irina. Her bubbly nature returned, and she adapted to her new life soon enough. Gone were the familiar surroundings that she had known since childhood. But the nine-year-old was soon her old self again and slipped into her new life. Watching Zaria's infectious smile gave Irina strength and quiet satisfaction. She loved returning home from work and hearing her parents being entertained by Zaria's talkativeness. She wanted Zaria to be in touch with her Indian side too and continued to tell her about Indian mythology at night whenever she could. She wanted her to identify with both worlds, to have a belonging in two places.

For the first few weeks, Zaria told her mother that she missed her friends in India a lot and e-mailed them. They hadn't fully understood why she had to leave. They were all just children. Tara, Gul and she had all promised to stay in touch and remain best friends forever.

Chapter 5

Zaria was soon attending school in Moscow. At the public school, the child made friends quickly and soon settled into her routine of ballet lessons at her mother's old ballet school. Her mother was very earnest that she continue to dance.

"It will lift your spirits. Your papa would have wanted us to go on," she said, her tone wistful, her eyes hopeful.

Irina had started teaching ballet at Olga's school so Zaria's lessons were free. Mikhail and Galya cared for their grandchild when Irina was away, and watched her resume her life. Zaria's initial shock at suddenly finding herself in a cramped flat as part of a neighbourhood with dirty brick walls and crumbling elevators slowly disappeared. Her cheerful nature returned gradually, and she went back to being her bubbly self. Her grandparents told her stories and made her laugh. Under their loving care and guidance, the child's heart began to heal, little by little.

She would come home from school and Galya would help with her homework. Galya told her that she should be proud that she knew both English and Russian.

"I bet most kids at your school can't even speak broken English," Galya said.

Irina told her parents that she was thrilled to see her daughter happy and energetic once again. She, however, clearly looked like she couldn't move on. Her spirit was crushed, mutilated. She juggled teaching ballet with being a waitress. She taught ballet every evening for two hours at Olga's school. Six mornings a week, except Sundays, she waited tables for long hours. She often came home only just before seven and Zaria would only see her during dinnertime for a few hours before she went on to her bartending job. She sometimes came home only after midnight, staying extra hours to make more money. She wanted to give her daughter a decent lifestyle.

One evening Irina took Zaria to see a ballet at the famed Balshoy Theatre. She'd got the tickets through Olga, who insisted that Irina take her daughter to watch a live ballet performance.

Zaria hardly realised how lucky she was to get the chance to see a ballet performance live. She had spent most of that afternoon crying, remembering her father and refusing to be comforted. Even as the show started, she was still trying to suppress her tears, as Irina sternly told her to stop and watch the stage.

When the curtains rose, Zaria stopped crying and watched curiously as the *Swan Lake* ballet unfolded in front of her awe-struck eyes. She saw the costumes, the sets, the lights and her eyes were transfixed. She watched the ballerinas leap across the stage—they looked like they were floating angels. When the ballerina playing Odette did her solo, Zaria thought she was so beautiful that she literally watched her with her mouth agape. She thought her movements were magical—so graceful and swanlike as she moved across the stage, leaped and twirled. For the rest of the show, she didn't speak but watched spellbound.

That was the day the child knew what she wanted to be. That was the day the dream was born inside her and took hold of her completely. The day she would first begin to fantasise about being a ballerina. She knew she wanted it more than anything else and resolved that she would work at her ballet classes diligently. She had nearly lost interest in them over the past few months.

As they walked out of the theatre, she told her mother that she no longer wanted to be a princess but wanted to be a ballerina instead. That earned her a smile and a pat on the head from Irina, who was preoccupied.

Irina found time to take her daughter to some parks on weekends whenever she could. The refreshing air and idyllic green lawns made them both enjoy nature for a few hours. They both chatted away, sitting on the cool, green grass, amidst the families seated on the lawns, some with young children of their own. Zaria was very friendly with children of her age that she saw there, and sometimes joined them, for a game of tag in the children's play area. Irina also took Zaria to her ballet lessons four times a week. They would take the bus to the ballet school and Irina would watch as Zaria practised her steps and twirled around in the bus. The girl loved others watching her. Some people would clap when she finished, remarking on how cute she was. She soaked in the attention and would even bow with a flourish.

"*Poka*!" she would say with a wave, saying goodbye to her mother outside the dance class, as she eagerly ran in. In the class, she worked on her spring points, port de bras and sautés putting all her efforts into her dancing. Amidst the darkness of losing her father and a strange new life so different, she found the light she needed in her ballet lessons. She loved them. Olga taught her batch, and noticed that Zaria had both talent and interest.

At night, Zaria would hear her mother crying quietly into her pillow as they slept in the same room. The child was quiet, for instinctively she understood that her mother was in pain. She told herself that she wouldn't bother her mother for anything, so she would be less hassled.

Irina wanted to teach Zaria ballet personally but didn't have the time or energy to do so. Zaria was a fast learner at her ballet class, gradually developing as much grace and poise as she had energy. Her mother told her to practise at home when she was free. Sometimes before dinner, Zaria would do a little performance of some ballet steps and when she finished her mother and grandparents would cheer.

Zaria's grandfather Mikhail would tell her stories while she sat by his feet. She listened in rapt attention, spellbound by his storytelling.

"Tell me more, *Dedushka*" she would urge him whenever he took a pause.

She loved listening to the details of his personal stories and anecdotes. She would sit by his rocking chair by the fireplace when it was too cold to go out, asking him more about what he knew. Mikhail told her of the Cold War, the time in which he was born and the events surrounding it. He told her about the genocide of Jews during the Second World War and the way his father had escaped from a concentration camp miraculously. He spoke of the fall of the Soviet Union when Zaria was just a few years old.

Zaria's friends would come over to play with her on some days and Galya would watch over them. Mikhail and Galya doted on their granddaughter, correcting her only when it was necessary. The child grew to love her ballet sessions more and more. She accepted her new life quickly and ballet was the brightest thing in it for her. She would practise her jetes and splits meticulously in the little flat sometimes, as soon as she was finished with her homework. On her feet were her ballet shoes which she considered her most precious possessions. The shoes were made of satin and were coloured in a shade of light pink. They had thin, delicate, cream laces and maroon ribbon straps. They clung to her little feet as she twirled, wanting to become a part of her.

Chapter 6

Time flew by quickly and Zaria was soon a fourteen year old teenager. She had grown into a very attractive young lady, whom the boys loved staring at. Her green eyes sparkled with verve and her light brown hair was combed carefully and worn in a soft, silky ponytail. Her figure was slender, her face pale and her cheekbones high. The restlessness and talkative energy had gradually faded turning her into a more mature, self-conscious teenager.

She sat at the 'Bistro' coffee shop, munching on her leafy garden salad. She loved the well-heated place and its casual atmosphere. The babble of students' voices blended with the aroma of coffee and muffins. Tables were filled with people who chatted in groups over coffee and snacks. Behind the counter, waiters in blue uniforms took orders from the long lines in front of them. Zaria spotted some classmates sitting at a table across the room and waved to them with a bright smile. She was in a good mood every single day. Her cloth bag with her ballet shoes and leotard rested carefully on the armchair between her and Natasha, who was eating chocolate ice-cream and chocolate chip muffins. Dmitry sat in the chair to her right with his skinny frame and baby-face. Both of them were Zaria's best friends at school.

"So…tell me how your date with Jean went," Natasha whispered, grinning at Zaria.

She had medium length brown hair and a thoughtful, mature face.

"Oh he is such a good kisser," Zaria said, leaning forwards.

"Louder. The whole café should hear all the details of your make-out session," Dmitry remarked, sipping his frappucino.

Zaria waved him off and continued describing her date in detail.

"But he can't make it to the movie with us because of some dumb football game. What is it with guys and football?" she complained, throwing her hands up and looking at Dmitry.

"You won't get it," he stated, leaning back.

The topic then turned to Natasha's gymnastics practice and then to nerdy Dmitry's part-time job as a lab assistant to a science professor.

"So, what's up with that weird lab co-worker of yours?" Zaria asked him, pushing a tomato around in her bowl.

As her friends yakked, she stared at the bright tube lights under which people sat in maroon vinyl armchairs, working on their laptops. She fiddled with a strand of hair, as she watched a couple cuddling. She wasn't like a typical high school teenager with time to have fun and party. Her ballet classes consumed a great deal of time every evening. She also did not have time for a part-time job to earn extra cash and so saved her pocket money carefully to hang out with friends. The fact that Moscow was very, very expensive did not help either. But she was focussed on her life's ambition—to be a ballerina.

At three o'clock she glanced at her watch and jumped up.

"Okay, guys I have to run!" she said, grabbing her ballet bag and jacket and rushing out the door.

She stood on the wooden floor in her pale pink leotard and ballet shoes, watching her reflection in the mirror. Tall mirrors stuck to the opposite wall and ballet barres stood below them. The ballet studio was very large. The walls were painted a light green that gave a homely feel to the air. Framed photographs of famous ballerinas were hung on the walls around the room, some former pupils who had gone on to become stars, both in Russia and abroad. Zaria knew her mother's picture hung somewhere too since she had been the biggest prodigy of the school. A pale yellow door at the back of the room led to a small dressing room and a bathroom. Wooden steps were on the front side of the room, where some parents sat when they watched their young children perform at school shows. On one corner of the steps, a number of bags belonging to students were piled up. Zaria's was an old, brown cloth bag amidst the others' more posh bags, including some designer ones. Her plastic bottle of energy drink was next to it. She was part of the grade six class which Olga taught personally.

"Pirouette, everyone," Olga stated with a clap of her hands from her plastic chair in front of the room. She sat with her legs crossed, her grey hair in a tight bun atop her head.

"*Odin, dva…*" Olga counted in her deep voice.

Zaria stood in preparation for the pirouette with her left leg in front of her right, both turned outwards. She sprung into her favourite step, raising her right leg and bending it as she turned clockwise. She balanced on the pointed toes of her left foot, which was raised off the floor and held straight as she spun. Her hips and shoulders had to be aligned. Her arms remained immobile and her eyes focussed on one point at eye level. Then she kicked out her right leg with the toes pointed before bending it at the knee again, for another twirl. She felt the tautness in her leg muscles and her thighs as she spun. The light from the long white tube lights shone down on them, as all of them went through their exercises diligently. Zaria felt her leotard stretch, the silky material clinging to her, accentuating her slim waist and figure, as she listened to the music from the CD player.

As they finished the exercise, Olga said, "Good," nodding her head.

Olga was a former ballerina who'd been a legend during the Soviet times. She was in her late sixties and her brown eyes looked at her students with a careful scrutiny as she corrected each girl's posture. Her face looked wise and her voice was a deep, soothing one which she raised only when necessary. She taught with a controlled firmness that inspired respect from all her pupils. She had been a star with the famous Marensky Ballet in St Petersburg and also Irina's teacher in her final years of training. Olga had given up ballet when she was in her early thirties to teach, something she said she had an immense passion for.

She knew just how to make each of her pupils get their technique right and perfect their style.

"Your legs must be like moonbeams, like soft ribbons, delicate. They cannot wobble like jelly!" she called out as everyone raised one leg.

As a kid Zaria had been very heavy landing on her jumps, until Olga corrected her.

"Zaria… you are not a buffalo. Think you are a cat, dear," she had said with a smile.

That had made Zaria correct her jumps and land lighter. Olga would sometimes even personally correct her pupils—demonstrating a beautifully pointed instep, holding their ankles, knowing just how to make everyone get their posture right. With her teaching wobbles stopped and people who landed off balance would find the perfect balance. Zaria found that Olga could help her break the bounds of what she thought were her limits.

Zaria finished another exercise of port de bras and then walked with the others to the benches for a short five minute break. During her ballet lessons she forgot her mother's struggles, their money worries and everything else. She felt a burning ambition inside her, the distant dream of being a professional ballerina calling out to her. She watched the autumn outside, the trees shedding their leaves and the sun's yellow orb in the sky. Olga's classes made her feel like she was in a sanctuary, her second home. She attended classes almost daily for nearly two hours. On most Saturdays she had pointe lessons for a few hours, when other teenagers her age went about doing fun things. But whenever she was at Olga's classes, she felt a sense of belonging that she never felt anywhere else. Even if the heater stopped working sometimes and everyone shivered in discomfort, she focussed on her dancing. The winter cold would be seeping through the stone walls and make the aching chill spread through their bodies, thin and clad in skin-tight leotards, but she hardly noticed. She would never miss a lesson unless there was a heavy snowstorm or torrential rainfall. The longing to be a professional ballerina had grown stronger each year inside her. Irina was thrilled at her daughter's ambitions and made sure Zaria was able to juggle schoolwork and dancing well. At home, Irina ensured Zaria didn't have to do any chores so that she could save her energy for ballet. She was the perfect mother, Zaria thought, not pushing her but doing everything she could to help her forward. Sometimes when she asked, Irina would give her specific tips to correct her technique.

Zaria sipped from her plastic bottle of Gatorade energy drink and chatted with the others. She was friendly with some other students, and things were quite relaxed, as not all of them wanted to be professional ballerinas. She listened to a girl talk about her recent holiday in Italy and felt like an outsider. Top class ballet lessons at this school cost quite a lot of money. Hers were luckily free since her mother taught there. Most girls here were from private schools and were much richer than she was. They wore branded clothes while she mostly lived in shirts that her grandmother stitched for her. But she had the drive to dance, more than the others. Olga had, in fact, told Irina that Zaria was made for her ballet shoes, was a born ballerina.

Olga's academy was one of the most prestigious in Russia, and was more than two decades old. Zaria knew she was very lucky to have the opportunity to study there. She didn't want to go to a full-time ballet school like her mother had. She wanted to have as normal a teenage life as possible. Irina had been to a full-time ballet school and had told her how stressful it was. Everything there was super strict. Students had to wake up early in the morning, dance everyday and do their schoolwork through correspondence along with it. Zaria thought it sounded too intense, for her at least.

After class, Olga shed her teacher persona and all the girls would sit around and talk to her. They were all in awe of her and of her various achievements over the years. They would ask her about her stage days and her travels to exotic locations. Olga would tell them everything—the hard conditions in the Soviet times, the dusty rooms with the peeling paint that they stayed in, the famous people she'd met, and so on.

"When my parents were children in St Petersburg in the time after the Revolution of 1917, conditions were horrible. Poverty everywhere, no food for anyone. No heat at home, everyone could die of the cold. People would be on the streets, looking through the garbage for a morsel to eat," she said, as her students listened enraptured.

The students in turn told Olga things about their lives, like they were friends. Zaria would talk to her about things at home and at school. She thought of Olga as her guiding light, almost like a second mother. She remembered her hugging all her students' goodbye when they were much younger.

After class, Zaria would walk outside with a few others towards the Moskva River that flowed nearby. Her friends walked the other way. She walked on alone to the bus-stop, humming along to the tune on her Walkman. Though it was hectic balancing school and ballet lessons, she did everything with a smile. That was her spirit. She had fairly good grades at school too, ones she wanted to keep up.

She didn't yet know where life would take her and wanted to just be carefree and enjoy the present, not think about her future. She stood waiting for the bus on the gravelly pavement, watching the river flow by, slowly, ever unhurried in its pace.

Her first major performance was when she was fifteen years old. She was part of the National Junior Ballet Theatre's production of the

Nutcracker. It was her first time on the professional stage but she danced well. After that, she performed twice a week with the group for ten performances. She had tried out for the part since Olga had urged her to audition. She had done so apprehensively, but was told that she was a talented dancer for just fifteen. Personally, she couldn't have been more thrilled at the compliment.

But in her love life she was very unlucky. She had gone on her first date when she was fourteen. They went to the movies and she had her first kiss. It had ended in just a few weeks though, when the boy was seen kissing another girl. Since then she had only dated one other person. Her ballet commitments left her with no time for relationships.

She and her mother visited India that December. Preethi and her husband had paid for their tickets saying that they really wanted to see them. Zaria was glad to be back in the city where she had spent her childhood, the best part of it, at least. Her best friends from her toddler years, Gul and Tara, were ecstatic to see her again. They took Zaria to a party that Tara threw one weekend.

Tara's house was very large with a huge front lawn. Teenagers were scattered across its breadth, their voices a murmur that blended with the loud, pulsating music from the DJ's corner. The multicoloured strobe lights moved across the wooden makeshift dance floor in the middle of the garden. A snack table stood on one side of the lawn with chips, cheese crackers, kebabs and other eatables. Plastic chairs were next to it, where some people sat and chatted.

Zaria wore a knee-length black skirt and a spaghetti strap blue top. She looked around and saw all her old friends from her Alpha School days. They all looked so much more grown up. Everyone greeted her warmly and said that she looked great. Some gave her hugs. She loved their friendliness. Many of her friends were very curious about her life in Russia and asked her lots of questions. She chatted with them for awhile.

"Let me remind you of our classmates since it's been so long. There's Devinder who is Ashwin's best friend," Gul said slowly, pointing to a tall boy with a beard who wore a turban on his head.

"And that's Gul's older brother Farhan. The three of them are such cricket nuts. And there's…" Tara added talking much more rapidly.

"Hey, I remember everyone. How could I forget? You guys have kept me updated on everything here through e-mail," Zaria said with a fond smile.

Tara wore a knee-length purple sleeveless dress and wore her hair in a short stylish do. Gul, who was a more modest dresser, wore white silky pants and a willowy green blouse. Zaria noticed the change in her two friends. Tara looked very different and her tomboyishness was completely gone. But her bossy, frank nature that Zaria loved so much was still there. Gul clearly seemed to have lost some of her shyness. She was still as sweet as ever, asking how Zaria and Irina were doing. She had long, wavy hair that fell to her waist, dark eyes and a very pale face. Zaria marvelled at how two people with totally opposite natures could still be best friends.

A tall, dark, curly haired guy walked up to her just then. It was Ashwin.

"Hey, Zaria! Wow, you're looking really pretty," he said.

Zaria laughed and gave him a hug.

"How are you?" he asked.

"I'm great," she replied. "And it's so amazing to see you all again."

Ashwin looked very different from the short, skinny boy she remembered who hardly said a word to her. He had grown very tall, had a deep tan and his curly hair was grown to below his ears. He and Zaria chatted together for a while. He asked her about her life in Moscow and she told him about the city and her friends from school. Tara pulled up a chair and sat down next to them when Zaria asked her to fill her in on everyone in Chennai. Tara told her about the boy in class she was seeing. She added that Gul with her beauty had lots of boys after her and was seeing a boy called Jai though her conservative parents would yell if they knew.

Zaria spent the rest of the evening on the dance floor, enjoying the company of her old friends. She realised fondly how happy she was to be back in the city of her birth, the place where her mother had known so much love and warmth.

Zaria hung out with Tara, Gul and their group of friends. Ashwin, Devinder and Farhan were also part of the same gang so she got to know them well too. She thought Ashwin was a really nice guy and she was soon good friends with him. He was also currently single and Zaria admitted to herself that he was cute. Yes, he definitely was.

Irina took her daughter to visit her paternal grandparents one day. Jaya gave her a kiss on her head, and clutched her tightly.

"Wow, what a beauty you've turned out to be," she said in the same voice Zaria remembered, admiring her at arm's length.

"Thank you *Paati*," Zaria replied with a large grin.

She noticed that her grandparents were cordial enough to her mother, but there was no warmth. The teenager did not know anything of the past, the reason for some awkwardness that she could easily sense. When she asked her mother about it later, Irina refused to talk, saying that the past belonged to the past and that she would not discuss it. Zaria did not press the issue, saving her questions for later.

Over the days, her grandparents gave her a large amount of money to spend apart from gifting her salwar kameez and ghagras. They pampered her so much, that Irina had to remark on it. Her aunt 'Preethi Athai' as Zaria always called her, had not only visited them in Moscow five years ago but had also been in touch with Irina on e-mail. Preethi had been unable to conceive and have the children she had wanted so badly but still tried to smile her way through life. Zaria had to admire that side of her, the spirit she still tried to keep up despite the severe ache.

Zaria had, since her move to Moscow at a tender age, thought of herself as almost totally Russian and hadn't given any thought to her Indian side until now. The memories of her childhood were faint but her mother told her of how happy she had been in Chennai, of how sheltered she had been. She soon found that she loved Chennai and felt a small connection to India and to the culture. They piqued her curiosity and she found she wanted to explore them further to see where it led. She loved the affectionate and welcoming nature of Indians, the way they made you feel at home. Soon, she quietly harboured a hope that she could visit again. Luckily for her, she had never felt an identity crisis in Moscow. Since she looked a lot more Russian most people wouldn't know of her Indian side until she mentioned it. But she now secretly found her Indian ancestry exotic and was glad to have that side to her.

Another thing she liked about Chennai was seeing her mother look relaxed and happy when she was there. Zaria did notice such things, young as she was. She was the half of the two of them that made the jokes, and wished she could see her mother this unperturbed more often. It was hard for Zaria to tell her best friends in India that her mother had to struggle as a waitress, but they were nothing but kind and sympathetic. They never discussed it at all. But some people in India could not understand that they were poor because of her father's name. Most of her friends from her posh private school in India were from upper middle class families and some from seriously affluent ones. Nobody had to work as a waitress. They could sit in spas all day long. Most mothers were high flying socialites and most of her friends had holidayed in London and New York. They wore branded clothes and travelled in swanky cars. *But at least we aren't on the streets,* Zaria heard her mother's voice echoing in her head.

Chapter 7

Zaria was now ready for college. Irina insisted that she graduate and get a degree before embarking on a full-fledged career in ballet.

"Sweetheart you can never be sure you'll make it in ballet. What if you don't? You don't know where life can take you," she said.

Zaria lost her temper at first and argued with her mother for hours, saying that she wanted to just finish her ballet training and dance. Irina screamed at her daughter and gave her a long lecture about being headstrong. Zaria soon saw how intense her mother was about the subject and understood how much Irina didn't want to ever see her in a position like hers. She needed a back-up plan if ballet didn't work out. Just in case.

"Economics would be a very solid, good degree to get," Galya said, "unless you are interested in something else. History?" she asked, peering at her from beneath her round, wire-rimmed glasses.

Zaria thought for awhile but they decided that economics made more sense. It would be useful and she liked the subject.

Irina was very firm on the topic of college and Zaria understood her logic. Making it as a professional ballerina was a very long shot at the moment. Though, honestly what she wanted to do was to just finish her training at a ballet school. It seemed to be the best springboard to a professional ballet career. She did, of course, know that her education was very important. Besides, two years at college didn't mean that she would have to put her dancing career on hold totally. She could continue to dance in the summer holidays, and she could continue to take part in competitions. If she juggled it successfully with her studies, nothing would be lost.

Moscow College was where she found herself that fall, when the leaves turned golden and fell gently onto the ground. It was a new chapter in her life. She was entering adulthood and stepping out into the world. College was a new, fun experience–making new friends, learning and letting go of the seriousness of dance for a while. Natasha was studying History at Moscow State University and Dmitry was studying Physics at the prestigious Moscow Institute of Science and Technology. They kept in touch but could see each other only rarely on some weekends.

Zaria was an attractive young woman now, no longer a school kid. She had her first lover that September–a panting blonde haired boy who said she looked like an exotic goddess with the touch of Indianness in her face and her sensuous green eyes. More boys followed though none were serious. She was too absorbed in training for summer shows and continued to attend her ballet classes on weekends. She also focussed on her studies, putting in full effort in her homework and assignments. She continued stretching in her dorm every day, to make sure her body didn't forget she was a dancer. If someone passed by, they would see her long legs stretched out in a split. In the summer holidays, she taught some beginner's ballet classes at Olga's school for pocket money.

New friendships were made. A boy at the college called Sasha was given the title of the ultimate joker within a few months of their starting the first year. He was tall, lean and wore his long dirty blonde hair in a new hairstyle every few months. He thought of himself as suave, and openly admitted to fantasising about every gorgeous woman on the campus. Sasha was very popular and was also known to be the biggest prankster.

One cool spring afternoon, a group of students sat on the campus lawns. Zaria was amongst them, trying to read a textbook. Sasha strutted up to them just then.

"Hey! Forget those dull books. I was just reading up on the internet about a really cool myth about Rasputin's penis. His was rumoured to be massively long–over twelve inches…lucky guy!" he said. He wore a deep brown French beret, jeans and a red shirt with a silver chain around his neck. He had a tattoo on his right arm and a silver stud in one ear.

"Why are we discussing the length of someone's penis?" Zaria asked, grinning.

"Okay, wait. Now I have some serious news. Guess what?" Sasha said, his arms held in the air.

"What? You are the best kisser or the best at…" another girl nearby said sarcastically, counting on her fingers.

"No, no, I'm serious," Sasha said, making people look up. "I… am going to try…" he continued dramatically, pausing for effect. Everyone set their textbooks down and looked at him.

"To break a Guinness world record!" Sasha finished.

"For what? Kissing the most girls?" Zaria asked sarcastically.

"Nah, I'm serious. There are lots of small, silly ones that I am going to try and break. If so many people can get in there for silly things like dancing for the longest hours, I too can definitely break some record," Sasha stated.

A boy called Edward stood up and said, "Look, I will bet you on this dude. If you can actually break one, because they are all very difficult to break, I will…"

"You, my friend, will have to wear a little black dress and sing opera on Tveskaya Street," Sasha said, concocting quickly.

"You're on!" Edward said. He and Sasha gave each other a high five as the rest of the students cheered.

For the next few years, Zaria would sometimes see Sasha doing ridiculous things. Once she saw him standing on one leg, with a huge crowd gathered around him. A professor stopped by, shook his head and walked away. The next week, he was trying to swat as many mosquitoes as possible on the campus. Then he started collecting pens, mostly from girls who giggled and gave it to him, but he gave up on that too. By the end of their two years in college, Sasha hadn't succeeded but said that he wouldn't give up for the next twenty years at least.

Zaria's two years of studying microeconomics, gold point fluctuation and making new friends flew by quickly. She felt a lot smarter at the end of her course, enriched with knowledge for life.

When she was done with college, she spent the next year completing her ballet training at Olga's school. She worked tirelessly in perfecting her arabesques, grand jetes and pirouettes. She learnt the duets and also had to learn some modern jazz dancing and basic folk dancing. Piano and voice lessons also had to be finished, along with studying French and the history of ballet. The zeal she had for ballet was thrown into her lessons in her pointe shoes.

Soon her training was complete. She was brimming with dreams and ambitions–to conquer the world which lay out there. The desire grew stronger every day. But could she make it?

Chapter 8

The young woman woke up and stretched when her alarm went off at 5:45 am. Still groggy, she forced herself to throw off the brown quilt covering her snugly, and cast her glance outside to see the bright flecks of sunrise filtering through the window. The sun was just rising, bathing the sky in a fast brightening saffron flush.

She stood straight before the mirror and did the morning stretches for her hamstrings and calf muscles. This had become a daily regimen as soon as she woke up. When she finished she went to check on her mother, but on opening Irina's bedroom door found her in bed with a man she had never seen before. They were entangled between the sheets, seemingly naked. Zaria felt surprise shoot up inside her and couldn't help staring at the strange man's dark hair for a moment. She then hurriedly shut the door and walked to the kitchen. Hmm, her mother had, of course, been dating again since some months ago.

She forgot, she had even spoken about it to her. But suddenly, Zaria felt very perturbed and glanced towards her mother's bedroom again. She felt a protective surge towards her mother, wanting to know who the stranger with her was, and yet not wanting to know him at all. Seeing her mother with someone else was still a little…well, hard to get used to. Her father's face sprung to her mind, the picture of her parents on their wedding day. She shook her head and forced herself to shrug off these conflicting thoughts for the time being and think about the day ahead.

She poured herself a bowl of corn flakes and hot milk, feeling the warm liquid wake her up. Usually, she just ate a light breakfast before rehearsals and sometimes had an apple along with it. She washed and dried the cereal bowl, glass and spoon and after putting them back in their places, went to her room. There she pulled on her deep blue leotard and skin coloured stockings, before slipping on jeans and a purple T-shirt on top. She climbed down the flight of rickety brown stairs to the floor below in her black sneakers. As she passed the neighbour's apartment, she waved to the elderly gentleman, a former Soviet soldier, who resided there. He was up early as usual and sitting in his rocking chair in his ground floor apartment, with his spectacles on. He waved back and smiled.

The fresh morning air was refreshing and slightly chilly as it hit her cheeks. She liked the brisk, healthy ten-minute walk to her dance school which was in the same neighbourhood. She needed the early start to the day, and her body had to get used to a certain routine. Hardly any noise could be heard in the area, where most of the residents rose much later. The Soviet style blocks of flats in the poorer neighbourhood were all made from panels. They were painted a dull yellow on the outside with white porches and pointed light brown roofs. A winding road curved alongside them, passing the small lawns with bushy green shrubs that each flat had. The area was a kind of sleeping village, far removed from the centre of the city.

Summer was the time of the year Zaria loved the most—more so because her friends were now free from their university courses to meet up with her now and then. But her chief priority was getting into serious shape for the upcoming ballet competitions she was going to take part in. Ballet was her first thought when she woke up each day.

She put her iPod headphones into her ears and was soon humming along to her favourite song—'*Don't stop me now*' by Queen. She walked on the side of the road, her shoes crunching on the hard gravel, while she took sprightly steps. A group of young kids from the neighbourhood were avidly kicking a football around the ground. She dodged the black and white ball that flew past her head with a laugh and waved to them.

She was now out in the real world. The thought of finally being free to dance full time flushed her with wild, expectant dreams. Her future lay ahead and for the first time she knew she had to think seriously about the road in front of her. She wanted to plan her first steps in the professional ballet world with deep and careful consideration. But could she secure a part with a group or would she never make it? She didn't know. The needles of disquiet were present in her thoughts, in a tiny space at the back of her mind. But she tried not to dwell on them and focussed instead on every plus point she had going for her—talent, confidence and potential. She knew she had strong ambition too, perhaps stronger ones than many hopefuls, and that had to mean something.

She wanted to take part in every single ballet competition possible until she won a place or got noticed. Olga had advised her to take part in a competition that would take place the following month in St Petersburg. Zaria had already started working on a short routine for the competition with Olga's guidance right from a few months before she graduated from University.

Every single day, she would rehearse the routine the way Olga had taught it to her. Her thirst to do well was present in every pore of her being. Also, since she had been learning and performing over the years, she had grown to love classical music. She greatly enjoyed listening to her mother's collection of Bach, Mozart and Beethoven, besides the scores from some famous ballets. Classical music existed along with rock and Bollywood tunes on her iPod playlists. She also wanted to be knowledgeable about ballet and read about it quite a bit, especially about the legendary Russian choreographer Jorge Ballinchine.

She walked along, as a Lamborghini and a Lexus zoomed past. She was in the city of billionaires, where she still felt very small despite being here for so long. She finally turned the street corner and arrived at the studio building, which had a tall fir tree growing on its right that nearly clung to it. Olga had kindly agreed to let her use one of the rooms in her studio for her morning rehearsals for the competition routine. Zaria didn't have a lot of space at home, though she had pushed a table in the sitting area to the corner and tried to practise there. The people who lived downstairs had complained of the noise as she jumped on the floor above their heads and been extremely grouchy in general.

She pushed open the tall, wooden door and walked in, shutting the door to the draft of the early morning. High windows against one wall opened out to a view of some small houses in the distance, with trees scattered around them. Zaria loved the look and feel of being in the studio, which had an air of aesthetic quietness to it. Even the minty air freshener that hung in the air was a smell she liked, just like everything else about Olga's school. She felt so much at home here, where her talents had been carefully moulded since a child. The room was very large, so she had ample space to work with. She could hear her footsteps resonating on the wooden floor as she walked across to a small steel chair near the bars. She placed her brown cloth bag on it, plugged in her mother's small portable CD player and pushed the play button.

As the soft piano melody glided out gently from the speakers, she warmed up, feeling her limbs stretch familiarly under her skin tight leotard. She relished having the chance to practise when there weren't any inquisitive eyes to watch her or judge her. Solitude did have its bonuses when she could also work with more focus on certain sections of her routine and rehearse them to perfection. Perfection was what she always aimed for. Also, Olga was willing to help her better her technique, which she felt Zaria could achieve with hard work.

Zaria had the room to herself for just exactly two hours and so began right away with some physical exercises. She did some jumping, abdomen crunches and exercises for her back and stomach first. Then she did some exercises with light weights attached to her left leg, an exercise that she did often to strengthen her ankle. She wanted to be at her fittest, and keep her body feeling strong. After the warm ups, she launched into practising the routine which Olga had taught her. She had rehearsed it daily in the winter, when they had both started crafting the routine whenever Olga could spare time from her teaching. The memory of when she had first set foot in Olga's dance school rushed back to her suddenly and made emotion overflood her. Her mother had led her forward by hand to meet Olga, her old dance teacher. Zaria had seen the former ballet legend smile at her with kind blue eyes, as though she was examining her, reading her mind. She had suddenly felt nervous about a new teacher and clutched her mother's hand a little tighter when Olga smiled at her. She couldn't help but smile back. She then looked around and saw lots of other little girls and a few boys who were also beginning their first lesson that day. She recalled how after only a few lessons she would show off new steps to her grandparents, prancing around their flat.

The music fell on Zaria's ears and roused the fire in her, as the flame began to burn. The song playing was *'Toccata in D minor'* which poured forth in symphonic piano notes. After the song finished she started practising her routine, doing the first few steps from memory and feeling attuned to the space she was in. Goosebumps filled her as she let the music enter her body, moving it along with the rhythm. Good music always made her perform with a lot more energy. As she danced she couldn't help daydreaming of her performing in the competition—the loud claps, the judges favouring her, winning a place. An almost impossible craving to win a place at the competition was within her, gushing into her veins. She desperately wanted to be a *somebody* and couldn't wait for it to happen. Not that she was just a total dreamer. Her discipline and commitment were as fierce as her drive.

For two hours, she laboured with an unwavering focus on her nearly three minute routine, replenishing herself with lots of water in between. Olga told her she was dancing it very well already, but Zaria wanted to dissect every step and polish every single bit. She loved the feel of the piece she was performing, and it gave her bliss, a rush from within her. As she did her steps over and over again, the outside world vanished. It was just her and the stage. The two of them entwined. It was only the dancer that existed. *The dancer*.

She watched her reflection in the tall mirrors in front of her as she danced, observing every finger and toe and arch in her body from the judges' point of view. The mirrors showed multiple coordinated reflections of her slim form, as she glided and pranced about the room. Her self-critical eye went into a rush of corrections, inwardly chastising herself for even a tiny mistake, anything that was not perfect. She toiled away until the sweat soaked her hair and skin, until her limbs ached, until her toenails bled from standing on point. But she never felt the pain. She never complained even once. For her it was all worth it, it was her life. She finished her routine and stared at herself in the mirror, sighing. Hmm, she was doing okay but the middle section could do with a lot more improvement.

Being a dancer required tons of perseverance and hard work, which was the bare truth. Zaria was fully aware of this fact and was more than ready to put in her entirety every single day. She was no longer in age group competitions and wanted to compare her dancing to the top ballerinas, who seemed to possess that natural flair for technique. They had the advantage of having trained at full time ballet schools from a young age. But, even if they had an edge over her in the race to the top, she was glad she hadn't attended one. Having the regular experience of being a school teenager had been cool for her. Life was above all to enjoy, especially when one was young.

Irina was thrilled her daughter still wanted to take up ballet professionally but had often told her not to get her hopes too high as they could be dashed cruelly.

"Only a tiny, very tiny, percentage of those who want to be in the arts actually make it," she told Zaria.

Zaria understood, though she didn't want to dwell on that unpleasant reminder for the moment. The ballet world was tremendously competitive and so many gifted, beautiful girls were out there aiming sky-high. But it didn't matter. She still wanted to be a ballerina. Through her college years, her mind hadn't wavered even an inch and she was sure her mother's dance genes lay inside her too. Her yearning to dance professionally hadn't faded or diminished but instead burned brighter now, more than ever before.

She charted out a daily workout routine for herself to ensure that she improved her fitness and stamina and also built the right muscles to make sure her body looked as good as was needed. Every day she woke up before six am and did an hour of Pilates, abdominal exercises and stretches. Some exercises were designed to specifically strengthen her back and stomach muscles. She also had an Achilles heel—literally. Her left ankle was rather weak and she had already sprained it once as a teenager. It was not an impediment to her dancing but she knew she had to be careful of hurting it once more. She did a few exercises specifically for her ankles that Olga had taught her. She also practised some yoga postures she had learnt from her aunt in India. Then she headed to the studio as usual to work on her routine, practising and practising until the sweat poured down her face and hair. She had to make it. She had to.

Three times a week, she walked to a public swimming pool which charged a very low entrance fee, and swam a few laps there to build her shoulder muscles. She also started working resolutely on shedding the excess weight she had gained. She had always been naturally slim but had put on a kilo or so during her college years. Irina and Olga rattled off a list of things she would need to eat. "Whole grains, cereals, fruits, vegetables, fish, poultry, nuts, dairy products, iron, proteins, vitamin A from egg yolks, leafy green vegetables, vitamin B1, vitamin B2,…" Olga said as Zaria jotted them down in a notebook.

The list went on. Zaria listened as Olga explained how she needed certain food groups for energy, building muscles and for maintaining healthy nerve cells. Zaria ensured that she followed her given diet plan very strictly. She had been off junk food, fatty foods and sodas since about fifteen but had allowed herself bites of the occasional chocolate cake on birthdays. When she had her summer holidays during college she had veered off her diet a couple of times. Now, however tough it was, she couldn't nibble on sweets even when she had a die-hard craving for an ice cream cone in the heat. Every meal she ate was in keeping with the required diet and she didn't take even a bite of anything that was prohibited. For ballet, no sacrifice was small or trivial.

In the ballet world, there was no chance of getting work if one wasn't slim. Russian ballerinas needed to look petite—small hips, breasts and butts. Irina however, warned Zaria that it wasn't worth becoming anorexic just because of the pressure of seeing thinner girls at auditions. She told her daughter stories from her dancing days about the dangerous eating disorders and drug addiction some dancers had become entangled in. Zaria watched her mother's concerned face and nodded, understanding her worries. She would never mention trying a drug or two at some parties during her late teens. Now, she was older and knew her body had to be handled with the utmost care. The impetus and the brutal ambition to make it were overpowering her. Her attitude towards her dancing regime became more serious than before. She had begun meditation, for a few minutes in the early mornings. It helped her thoughts flow and made her realise certain emotions which lay buried deep inside beneath prickles of doubt. Olga had instructed her to try meditating to get over her impatience.

As the weeks went by, she looked at herself in the mirror and watched her stomach get slightly flatter thanks to the abdomen crunches she did daily. Thankfully, she had stopped growing at five foot six, though her father had been over six feet. She wouldn't need to mention that extra quarter inch in her height. Ballerinas who were too tall wouldn't really fit in, since they couldn't tower over their male partners. On the plus side, Zaria was gorgeous, her facial features giving her the typical Russian beauty look, with her pale, creamy skin. Her eyes were very green with long lashes and thin eyebrows. Her nose was small and so was her chin. Her cheekbones were sculpted high and her cheeks filled out when she smiled. Her lips were full and pink and her neck long, like her legs. Her waist was tiny as was needed and her figure was like a model's. On the whole, she looked almost totally Russian but the slight Indian tint was just barely visible in her face.

"You have immense discipline and passion to succeed. Those are just as important as talent," Olga said to her one afternoon.

Zaria nodded and felt pleased to hear from her teacher that she had that quality in her.

Alongside her exuberant pursuit, the thought of not fulfilling her dreams of being on stage pained her. Working at an office desk was the last thing in the world she wanted to do. But many girls who were exceptional dancers hadn't been able to make it into any ballet group. After all, there were hundreds of girls who graduated from ballet schools in Russia every year, many nearly perfect in their technique and ready to do almost anything to start rising. But Zaria didn't let that scare her. She knew she had a chance too.

Tragedy struck Zaria's family very harshly one day. Her grandfather Mikhail was diagnosed with a brain tumour. The doctors told Galya that they couldn't save him and that he had a few months at the most. They were all in shock at the news that they were so unprepared for. Zaria cried and blurted out that she didn't want to take part in the competition anymore. Galya and Irina consoled her and said that she had to go on with it and do her best for the sake of her grandfather.

Zaria finally calmed down and promised them that she would do just that, to make him proud.

It was a few days before she could get her mind to concentrate fully on her practice once more. She resolved to give the competition two hundred percent of her efforts. Then, just eighteen days before the competition, she suffered another setback. She twisted her left ankle slightly, and had to rest it for three whole days. She panicked, thinking it wouldn't heal in time for the big day. She had practised the routine enough times, so she could still go on. Olga told her to just rest for a few days and assured her that it would be alright.

Day after day, she felt the trepidation and tension mount. Could she give her best or could she not? There was no way she could back out now.

Thankfully, her ankle healed in time and she returned to normal practice a week before the big day.

The competition was very famous and very prestigious, but not open to professional ballerinas and dancers who had already been contracted to companies. It was the 8th International Ballet Competition and was held once every two years in St Petersburg. Aspiring dancers regarded it as the World Cup of ballet. Previous winners had become national celebrities, some being invited to finish their training at the most illustrious schools in the country. Some had been discovered by directors who watched the competition and had been asked to join ballet companies straightaway. Zaria knew that if she put up a strong showing at this one she had a very solid chance of breaking through. Over a hundred dancers from different countries around the world would be participating in it. Zaria had made the cut in the age group of nineteen to twenty two, after getting through the auditions held the previous month.

She stood backstage, stretching and awaiting her turn. She had taken the train to St Petersburg alone, telling her mother that she wanted to do it that way. Irina had since sent her many confidence boosting text messages, wishing her luck and telling her not to lose heart if she didn't do well. Zaria had taken some painkillers for her ankle and was glad it didn't feel sore. As she sipped from her bottle of energy drink, she thought back to the first competition she had taken part in when she was nearly fifteen. She clearly recalled how nervous she had been. And how she had messed up a few steps of her routine because of it. But when she was seventeen she had secured second place in one competition and subsequently received the offer to train full time at a prestigious ballet school. She had been confused since she didn't want full time training at that age. She wanted to enjoy her remaining months in school and wasn't sure if she would even make it in the professional ballet world. The opportunity did seem too good to refuse and the thought of going into ballet full-time was enticing, but her mother insisted that she complete her education. Zaria soon felt the same way. Who knew if she didn't make it, or didn't like the ballet world as much as she thought she would? She didn't want to be a dot in the sea of aspiring dancers, who never got parts despite being fantastic. She finally saw what her mother meant, as the highly competitive ballet world couldn't answer everyone's dreams.

Zaria pulled out the large, oval mirror she carried in her bag and inspected her face. Eyes with thick eyeliner, heavy mascara and pale eye shadow stared back. She'd done her own makeup, and it was surprising she had pulled it off when she hardly knew how to do it. A friend of hers from Olga's school had lent her lots of professional makeup. Zaria had practised putting it on only a few times and wasn't good at it. At first she'd just stared at the many brushes and tubes before her, not even knowing what was what. Irina had slowly and patiently taught her how to apply the makeup, demonstrating strokes with the brush. Looking in the mirror, she suddenly wished her mother had done her makeup that day. It was clear from her reflection that she had done a very mediocre job. She touched up the light pink blush on her cheeks. Her hair felt so heavy, with the innumerable pins she had shoved into her bun. Her lipstick didn't seem to be even and her foundation seemed patchy and a shade too light. But there was no time to set anything right now. She kept her fingers crossed that her fake eyelashes wouldn't fall off as she danced.

The announcer's striding voice over the microphone called out another name and that distracted her from her thoughts. The competition required participants to perform a specific one and a half minute solo variation of *Esmeralda*. Zaria went over her routine again and again in her head and recalled all the things Olga had told her to be careful about. Amongst all the other participants backstage, most accompanied by their coaches or mothers, she kept to herself. She sat all alone on a wooden bench, trying to tune out the many voices around her. The scents of so many kinds of perfumes were in the room and she realised with a groan that she had forgotten to bring some. She probably stank and smelt terrible, but what could she do? Her red costume was new and it fitted her well, although it felt a little too tight near her chest. She sat down and put on her ballet shoes. She tied the ribbons slowly and carefully—over her foot, round the ankle and to the back again. Then she took the second ribbon over the first and round her ankle. Finally, she tied a knot on the inside of her ankle and tucked the ends of the ribbons in as neatly as she could. She took a deep breath and then did the same for her left foot.

As the competition continued, she fidgeted with her hands and glanced at her watch. Then it was her turn before she knew it. She danced the variation of the *Esmeralda* piece and put in her best, the nervousness not visible as she performed with every ounce of energy. The music flowed and she did all the steps she had learnt, ones she had practised to death. She finished her routine and then bowed, shooting a dazzling smile to the judges. As she walked offstage, tiny qualms started knocking at her but she shoved them far away. She had done okay, she thought. Yes, she had felt good out there. Not that that meant she could make it through to the next round. Or perhaps she had done better than she thought? She knew she needed to be realistic now. She had done what she could and the rest was in the hands of fate.

When the results came out, she was overjoyed.

She made it to the final round of the competition!

Two days later, she headed again to the famed theatre in St Petersburg which was the home of the Marensky Ballet—one of the most illustrious ballet companies in the world. She walked into the theatre alone, once again having asked her mother not to accompany her. She wanted to get used to going to competitions and auditions by herself, as she planned to go to every possible one she could from then on.

As she waited her turn in the wings, her heart blazed with an innocent optimism that her routine would be well received. Most of the other finalists had come with their coaches and she heard them receiving last minute tips. She tried to tune out from the Russian voices—some loud, some quiet. Her solitary figure started doing warm up stretches, breathing deeply and trying to calm herself. Her costume was a brand new one that she had purchased with money she had saved over the past few years. The tutu was red above the waist with black and silver sequins on it and the skirt was light pink, giving her a womanly and bouncy look, much like the variation piece she was going to perform. She slipped her feet gingerly into her light pink ballet shoes which she had washed and dried. She then slowly tied the laces around her ankles and tied the straps. She had done this thousands of times, but this time she deliberately took longer doing it. When she finally finished tying the laces, she felt the customary snugness in her feet. The magnitude of the occasion suddenly struck her.

She sat with her back straight and started to think about the competition once more. The judges consisted of a very famous former ballerina from the Balshoy, a director of the Moscow Star Ballet Company and another famous ballerina from Germany. The audience comprised mostly of schoolchildren and parents of some participants, besides some fervent ballet enthusiasts.

Zaria waited for her name to be called, listening to the claps as other participants finished their routines. As every minute elapsed, she felt her expectations mount. She was more enthralled than she was nervous.

Her turn came, sooner than she wanted it to. She went out on stage and performed with a bright smile, feeling confident and dancing like it was just another of the many competitions she had entered. The music from the CD thankfully played without any glitches. Zaria felt the prominence of the moment and she danced in fine form, her long limbs moving naturally on the unfamiliar stage. She lifted her leg straight and high above her head, smiling consciously. Later she managed a series of pirouettes without losing her balance. She got claps when she finished them. She finally ended the piece down on her knees and generous applause broke out along with some wolf whistles. She smiled widely, feeling she had performed really admirably. The infinite practices had really done what they were supposed to do.

She strode backstage, patting herself on the back for a great show and for committing no mistakes. That was all that mattered. She didn't want to think of the results, but knew that without some she would remain stuck in the middle of nowhere.

But destiny had unexpected things waiting for her.

The judges must have been tremendously dazzled, because she was placed third in her age group!

She felt a mix of both head-spinning euphoria and excitement. The third place would look fabulous on her resume. The girls who had been placed first and second were not Russian—one was from Ukraine and one was French. She felt buoyed that amongst the Russians in her group she had been placed the highest. This meant that she was really good, that amongst all those girls she had stood out! She felt much more relieved than happy, strangely, and felt a burst of conviction inside her. The next audition she went to, she was sure she would dance with more self-assurance. The third place was so, so very dear to her. It was her biggest achievement so far. She let the news sink in and let her brain cells try to absorb it. Third place. Wow!

Backstage, she was gathering her things, when a hefty middle-aged woman with lots of grey in her blonde hair walked up to her.

"Hello, I'm a director with the Moscow Star Ballet Company," the woman said, stretching out her hand to Zaria.

Zaria wasn't sure if she had heard right but shook the lady's very firm hand, not letting her disbelief play across her face.

"I watched everyone perform today and you were really good," the woman continued in a business-like tone.

Zaria was still unable to process what was happening. A director of a group thought she was good? She knew she hadn't even spoken a word to the woman and thought she must look foolish standing with her arms by her sides and not being more composed. But it seemed the director wasn't noticing any of it. The woman hardly showed any emotion on her stern, bespectacled face as she continued in her stiff voice.

"We need new talent, with good technique and beauty. You are someone we could use," she finished without showing a trace of emotion.

Zaria nearly gasped but caught herself just in time.

"When?" she asked simply, her eyes widening as she stood up straighter.

The director told her the date for the auditions for their next show that would run that winter. She then turned and walked off before Zaria could even thank her.

Zaria kept standing there, unable to comprehend what had just happened. Had she actually been asked to audition for a company? Someone had noticed her? Like some enchanted dream come true before she had even expected it? Could this be the chance that she would be able to grab? Or not? The Moscow Star Ballet was a group she had heard of, of course. It consisted purely of Russian dancers, so that was the reason she had been spotted over the winner and runner-up of the competition who were non-Russians. She couldn't help beaming as she packed her things, not even able to close her mouth for a second. She sauntered out of the theatre with a new spring in her step. Her break had come sooner than she hoped, and she wasn't going to waste it.

The big bad world of dance. She was ready for it.

Chapter 9

Zaria's mood was more jolly than usual over the next few days, as she prepared for her audition and also hung out on weekends with her friends. Dmitry was near to finishing his course in Physics and Sasha was studying further and intending to go on to law school while continuing with his record breaking obsession. Natasha was hoping to do some teaching work when she graduated and eventually go on to business school. Everyone had a different path, a different life, Zaria thought. And she had hers too. Even if it wasn't like everyone else's, it was certainly unique.

Some groups put out advertisements in a certain paper when they wanted new dancers and she would tirelessly go over them to see if she met their requirements. She kept an eye out for other auditions for ballet groups in Russia that were announced on one website. She looked up the audition requirements for the one she was called to by the Moscow

Star Ballet director. She seemed to fit the physical requirements—the height, weight and face they needed for the audition. Good thing she had lost weight, a few months ago she might not have made the cut. She paid the registration fee and then got down to preparing for the audition with focus. Under Olga's guidance, she primed herself for the audition, working on her technique assiduously. As the day of the audition drew nearer, she felt stress and rigidity pop up inside her alongside the eager hopes of impressing, the agony of not.

She took the bus to the Moscow Star Ballet Theatre that evening. She first peeked and then walked smoothly into the rehearsal hall where the audition was being held. The pastel walled room was packed with dozens and dozens of hopefuls, stretching and standing quietly, barely speaking at all. The feeling of fierce, cutthroat competitiveness hung in the air and she was sure it was in every girl present.

She waited her turn in line, looking at the girls around her, some younger, some older, some so skeletal that she could see the bones in their arms. She could smell the bloodthirsty urge to win in the air as they all waited. The number assigned to her, the one she wore on her back was the number thirteen. A bad omen. The black paper felt uncomfortable on her back, feeling like it would hinder her. A harsh sign to start off the audition, she thought, toying with her hair. Bad luck number. But she couldn't do anything about it.

When it was her turn, she performed her audition. She stood with a group of twelve and followed the choreographer's demonstrations, as the pianist played the accompaniment. Her eyes and ears observed minutely and she did the steps just as instructed. They were asked to demonstrate pirouettes and jumps besides some other things she wasn't very prepared for.

Despite number thirteen, she went through to the next round.

She was relieved and prayed that the next round went well too, that she didn't get kicked out. When the round came, she followed the choreographer precisely once again as she showed off her talents amongst the two dozen other girls around her. They all had to take turns in dancing a duet with the male lead, who had already been chosen.

As the auditions proceeded, the thirst to triumph showed in Zaria's dancing, the mad obsession with getting the part.

And it paid off, for she made the final shortlist of three girls for the part of the Sugar Plum Fairy in the famous *Nutcracker* ballet.

She stood waiting in her pale pink leotard, in the tall ceilinged audition room. The other two hopefuls stood on either side of her, the bright lights covering them all. They were inside the famous Moscow Star Ballet theatre, the birthplace of so many stars. Where talented Nobodys became Somebodys. Three company directors sat at a rosewood table in front of them. Zaria could hear her breath as she consciously breathed in and breathed out. She felt sweat sluggishly trickle down her forehead, but didn't wipe it away. Was her perfume too heavy? Her brown hair was in a meticulously done bun with a silky hair-tie. Her feet sweated inside her ballet shoes. She saw the stern looking grey haired former ballerina whispering furiously to the man next to her. Did they think her jetes weren't good enough? She shuffled in her new pointe shoes on the wooden floor. This was *the* moment. To her life without ballet was like lifetime in prison. She could never accept that. Ever. She glanced at the round clock that hung above the director's heads. When would they know? She pictured herself bowing regally, as dozens of roses were thrown at her feet. But to an observer, her face wasn't readable. She looked like she was just waiting for the bus. Her foundation felt so thick. The stony faced man shook his head. She moved her eyes to her right. The blonde had enthralled the directors. Zaria had felt such envy when she had seen her perfect pirouettes. She would surely get the part. She swallowed and then strained her ears to hear what the directors were saying. She prayed fervently, that they would like her. If she didn't make it, would she ever breakthrough and get a role in any ballet?

All the years of hard work may never materialise. What if she never made it, and just auditioned for years until she was forced to hang her shoes up wistfully? It would always remain a delusion. The directors were certainly taking their time. They were conversing in hushed tones, in rapid Russian. Then suddenly they stopped whispering and sat up straight in their tall chairs. The jury was going to announce their decision. Was she going to be eliminated? She looked at the grey haired lady with spectacles and swallowed. *Please let them say I was good, she thought. Please.*

The stony faced man in the centre spoke first. He looked at the blonde girl with great interest.

"You were really very good. Perfect twirls," he said to her, nodding. "We think you are the best choice for this part."

The minute Zaria was home she ran into her room and locked the door. No one was home. Thank God.

An empty glass stood by the bed. Picking it up, she flung it across the room. She screamed as it hit the wall and shattered. Her cheeks were red, flushed with anger. Then the tears finally broke free. She collapsed on the bed face down, sobbing. She cried for hours until her head felt like it would break open.

It was the end of the world. She may never come so close to getting a part ever again. And she was too proud to take her mother's help to be part of a group, something which could be done with just a few phone calls.

For three days, she did not leave her room. Locked indoors, she barely spoke, much to her family's alarm. Her thoughts were dark, as she imagined a black, bleak future. The pictures made her tremble and then cry some more.

Then came the phone call that was to change her life forever.

"We have to inform you of this, since you were the second choice for the role…" the official voice stated.

Zaria pressed her cell phone closer to her ear.

"The girl Natalia, who was chosen for the part, has declined it. She has taken up a bigger offer from the Marensky Ballet in St Petersburg. So we would like you to..."

Zaria could barely believe her luck as she learned that she was to take over the role.

Irina had actually advised her daughter to try and join this very group—the Moscow Star Ballet. The group was a city based ballet company, which had a small number of dancers but boasted a repertoire of critically acclaimed ballet shows. It was privately funded and had a relatively smaller budget than the country's more famous theatres but was famed for discovering new talents—many of whom had gone on to become sensations. They actively encouraged younger dancers who were in their early twenties and were constantly on the lookout for new faces. But serious talent was needed to get in and the bosses obviously thought Zaria had it.

The Sugar Plum Fairy. Sounded so nauseatingly sweet. That was the part Zaria was going to play in the reputed *Nutcracker* ballet. She'd been told by the directors that her exotic beauty was a plus point. Okay, great! So she had that over some others. The slight Indian tinge to her features wasn't a setback, but had instead succeeded in getting the directors' attention. Awesome.

Rehearsals would only be starting after about two and a half months, so she had some time off until then. She continued to polish her dancing daily. Being part of a group so quickly was surprising for her. But she wanted to stay there, do well and hopefully get a contract for a few years at the company. The dancers had just two and a half months to rehearse for the premiere and she was determined to create a stir right from the first day.

The fact that she was now part of a real company made her feel like a child opening a bag of magical wonders. She was punctual at all rehearsals, and followed the choreographer's and director's instructions diligently. She enjoyed the process, and being with a whole group of dancers was a different experience. She must have been all right in rehearsals at the beginning, for the choreographer didn't have reason to scream at her. In fact, she developed a relaxed vibe fairly soon, forgetting that it was her first role with a professional company. She brought to rehearsals all the ardour for ballet she carried within her.

Most of the other dancers in the group wove a web of reserve around themselves. But Zaria did get the chance to chat with some of them during rehearsal breaks. They all said they liked the group and confirmed the fact that it sincerely encouraged newcomers, and that some dancers had gone on to be a part of bigger companies—like the Balshoy Theatre. Where Zaria would do anything to be at one day. Her secret desire.

She had just ten minutes before she had to go on stage. No one was there to tell her when to be ready, she just had to know. One of the few backstage volunteers, a skinny, large eared young man, told all the dancers to get to the wings hurriedly as he ran back and forth checking things. Zaria looked at the pictures of her father and her late grandfather Mikhail in her purse for a few moments, feeling the tears well up at their never being able to see her perform.

Memories of her father came rushing to her when she looked at his picture. His sudden death had been the beginning of her mother's dark years of turmoil, the gaping void in her mother's life that still refused to close. Her mother had told her of that dark day in Diwali only when she was thirteen and had insisted on the details. Then too, she had told her only the bare facts of the death and nothing about the events that led to them returning to Moscow. Much as Zaria wanted to push them away before her big moment, the memories came unbidden and crowded her brain before she could stop them.

Diwali, the festival of lights arrived in November, lending an air of light and festivity to Chennai. At the Krishnans' home, many relatives and cousins came over for the celebrations. Zaria clearly loved Diwali and the bursting of all kinds of crackers during the festival. She wore a *pavadai,* the long skirt that young girls wore on traditional occasions. Hers was a pink one with gold-patterns and she wore matching gold earrings. She held sparklers in her hand, watching them sparkle at the ends and marvelled at them along with her second cousins. Their dog Jerry was scared of the noise, like all dogs, so they had to keep him in the room at the back of the house, where he couldn't hear too many bangs and blasts. Irina wore a peach silk embroidered sari and played the perfect hostess, beaming and interacting with all the guests with poise. Most of their relatives chatted together about family matters, while all the kids played together. The sound of laughter and conversation filled the house. Irina felt a special feeling of warmth and comfort in India at times like these.

Kolams and colourful *rangoli* adorned the floor outside the house. Burnished brass lamps had been lit, the flames flickering brightly and spreading their warmth throughout the house. Zaria and her young cousins stood outside, watching crackers being burst. They drew patterns in the air with their sparklers. The sounds of crackers bursting enveloped the town. Multicoloured lights exploded across the night sky.

"Diwali is celebrated because Lord Krishna killed the evil *asura* Narakasura," Zaria said to some of the younger kids, who were impressed. Irina smiled and shook her head, seeing that her child loved showing off her knowledge to others.

Rajiv was away making the obligatory courtesy calls at the houses of important business associates and some government officials. He was to join them in half an hour for the festivities.

Irina and Preethi were planning a surprise party for Rajiv's birthday the next month. They were both sitting down in the veranda discussing their plans for the bash.

"We have to draw up a guest list and ensure that all his favourites from the family and friends' circle are free that day," said Irina.

Just then she heard the phone ringing. She walked over to it and picked up the receiver, unaware as to how the call would change her life forever. A voice she didn't recognise at once spoke in a very sober tone.

"Madam, I'm sorry to tell you this, but I have some very unfortunate news. Your husband has been in a car accident. He was rushed to the hospital immediately…"

Irina suddenly felt the world stop. Was that her running or was she in a reverie? She could barely feel her limbs but she found herself in the car with Preethi, zooming to the hospital.

"Oh no! Oh no!" Irina cried, her heart pounding faster and faster. Tears blurred her eyes. No, it couldn't be happening! It had to be a nightmare, that's what it was. She felt like she was moving without consciousness, without feeling. Her throat felt constricted, she had to force herself to breathe.

They were soon outside the hospital Emergency Ward, where Rajiv's secretary stood, waiting for them.

His face was solemn as he said, "He was on his way back home. The car collided with a speeding truck…"

Irina could barely process his words. She collapsed into a chair nearby. Her body shuddered with anxiety. Preethi, who was in shock as well, gathered herself, and tried to console Irina. Irina put her head in her hands, unable to speak. She vaguely heard Preethi saying *shlokas* next to her.

Five minutes later the door to the Emergency Room opened and a doctor in a white coat came out. Irina and Preethi jumped to their feet as he walked towards them. His grave expression couldn't have made things clearer.

"Ma'am… I'm so sorry. We couldn't save him," he told Irina quietly, his eyes sad and serious.

Irina couldn't hold on anymore. Was that her screaming? Preethi helped her sit down and then went back to talk to the doctor. Irina clutched at her hair and wailed while the tears gushed out. The world had ended. Her head spun. She felt so faint. Her mind was burning and yet frozen. The man she loved had been ripped from her. He was really gone. *Dead*. Her world was crumbling. The antiseptic smell of the hospital was making her nauseous. She heard the fatality of death ringing in her ears. The chair underneath her felt cold and then she felt as though she was falling, falling and couldn't stop.

Hundreds of mourners attended the cremation, many wailing at the fact that their beloved Rajiv was gone. Zaria and her mother held hands as they sat together. Relatives with tear-stained faces were everywhere, whispering softly amongst themselves. Zaria cried a little, but was mostly quiet. Irina knew that her young mind could barely understand how her father had been plucked from her. The corpse, the face bandaged so fully that hardly any part of it was visible, lay in front of them. Irina cried quietly while she clasped her daughter's hand firmly.

Zaria snapped back to the present when she heard the sound of footsteps rushing past her door. She closed her eyes and thought of God for a brief moment She hadn't ever been religious, since her parents were from two different faiths themselves. Irina had been to a synagogue that very morning to pray that her daughter's big day went off without any glitches. Zaria knew how much of a role her mother had played emotionally in supporting her through auditioning and getting the part, her first role after college. As a college student she had a really minor role as one of the swans in *Swan Lake* with a small group. She got to perform that part fifteen times, in December that year. But this. This was so much bigger. She thought of how prestigious it actually was to be picked for the part of the Sugar Plum Fairy. Zaria had beaten over a hundred girls, many of whom were years younger. She was glad that her daily practice and workouts over the last few months had helped her immensely. Her mind was now more confident and it showed in her dancing.

Her makeup looked all right, considering she had applied it herself. The group had no budget for make-up artists and all the dancers had been taught about applying makeup professionally at a workshop and left to do it themselves. She felt her tutu stretched thinly across the skin of her body, caressing all the bones and curves. The costume felt like it was made just for her, as though it had been waiting for her to step into it. It completed her. When she wore it she felt like she morphed into another avatar, the dancer's spirit unleashed.

She took a deep breath, stood up and walked through the open wooden door to the wings of the large stage. This was her first real test.

She danced to the music, and gradually felt her large knot of tension taper away and then fade. She performed with everything she possessed—the aspirations, grace and the years of learning. She became someone else, with the dancing and the different expressions in her body. This was her chance to shine, amidst the others around the stage. In her light pink costume, she played her part conscientiously as the hot stage lights beamed down on all of them.

The story was of Masha who was gifted a doll shaped like a nutcracker by the magician Drosslmeyer. Later the nutcracker changed into a Prince. The prince was played by a young ballerina who wore a royal looking red and gold outfit. Masha and the prince then travelled to the land of Sweets ruled by the Sugar Plum Fairy.

The sets had a huge Christmas tree with multi-coloured as well as festive decorations. Special effects included a white bed that glided across the stage, supported by invisible wires. Most of the dancers wore light coloured tutus and they managed to project the overall effect of a popular children's tale, which it was.

Zaria did her solo bit. Her eyes looked out at the half full audience, mostly in darkness and shadows, but all watching. She could feel the eyes of classical dance lovers on her. Perhaps some were critics. What would they think? Those thoughts were soon forgotten as the dance went on and the self-consciousness blurred. So many people watching, it felt amazing. When she stood on stage with the other characters, she felt like she was really in the story and living it. As the harmonious composition filled the stage, that wonderful sensation of performing she loved to experience took over and gave her the electricity she needed. She finished her routine confidently, without a mistake. Her right arm had been stretched too much on that last step, but no one seemed to have noticed. Applause flowed generously as her solo finished and she struck a pose. The sound of the appreciative clapping was the most gratifying thing to hear.

The story progressed and everyone danced their parts, adding to the blocks of the tale. A celebration of sweets from around the world was produced. Zaria had to also dance a duet which she managed to do even better than her solo. After a final waltz, Masha and the prince were crowned rulers. And then the ballet ended. As the blue velvet curtains drew together slowly, all the dancers walked off stage into the wings.

Zaria thought she had done well. She felt a sense of colossal satisfaction, even delight at pulling it off. She muttered a "Well done" to the lead ballerina as she walked to the dressing room, but the woman acted like she didn't hear her and was already inside. Zaria forgot she wasn't in school anymore. The gracious niceties weren't always returned.

Zaria rushed down to the newsstand a few days later, when she heard that a review of the show had just come out that morning. She had pulled on a coat over her pyjamas and had barely brushed her hair in her hurry.

She pulled out a copy of the *Moscow Daily* from the newsstand and paid the vendor the roubles she had kept handy. The babble of shoppers walking out from the small grocery store in front of her and the low whir of passing vehicles barely fell on her ears. A woman glared at her and pushed her aside roughly. Zaria shot her a rude look and the woman grumbled loudly, saying that Zaria was blocking her way. Ignoring her, Zaria stepped aside clutching the newspaper and flipped immediately to the arts review page. She swallowed when she found the article at the bottom of the page with the headline "*Nutcracker* by the Moscow Star Ballet" in bold black print.

Below that the subtext read: "Enchanting and enjoyable." *Wow.* Her eyes flew over the article as she scanned it right from the top.

The critic had given it an upbeat and positive review, calling it "*one of the best shows by the company in months.*" The girl who played the main part of Masha was praised as "*superb, exquisite...*"

Zaria pushed her twinge of jealousy aside while wishing she could have been written about like that. She skimmed down a few paragraphs and froze when she saw her name in print. She could hear her own loud breathing from her throat. Her heartbeat seemed to stop.

"*Zaria, the newcomer playing the Sugar Plum Fairy, is a notable new talent with her graceful technique.*"

Oh Wow! Graceful. The reporter had said her solo could have been better, but all Zaria thought about were the compliments. She found herself grinning and then laughing aloud as she read the words again, her face brightening as if a torch had illuminated it.. She squealed. She jumped up and down with a humungous grin showing all her teeth and the people around gave her weird looks. But who cared? The critic thought she was good!

"Oh, my darling, I am so, so proud..." Irina said when she read it for the second time. She cut out the article and had it framed, and it soon hung in Zaria's room on a brown pinboard next to her cupboard.

For days and weeks, she played the part of the Sugar Plum Fairy, the stage becoming more familiar to her with each passing day. Every positive word of encouragement from the director and from Olga gave her more belief in the fact that she could go further. Olga had watched her dance once and had called her up to say "My dear, you have improved so much. I can't tell you how proud that makes me..."

Those words were revered in Zaria's mind, the words of her favourite teacher. After all, what if she had messed up on her first major stage run? Life barely gave you second chances. And that could have made her fantasy of being on stage for years turn to hot, black ash. Scary to even think about.

Zaria's college classmates had gone their separate ways, though she was in touch with most on Facebook and e-mail. Some were going on to other universities and some were working at jobs already. Dmitry was going off to the prestigious Massachusetts Institute of Technology in America to continue his scientific route while Natasha was heading off to Ukraine. She was following her heart since her boyfriend was there, and she was planning to do an MBA in Kiev some years later. Sasha was aspiring to be a corporate lawyer as well as currently tweeting about his mad attempt to break a Guinness world record for trying to collect the largest number of women's bras. He had given up on his attempt to roll an orange on the ground with his nose for the longest distance. Such silliness, but the world needed more such characters.

Zaria was climbing a different stairway, treading a different trail, feeling the exuberance of getting off to a positive start. The nights that she spent performing, leaving her too tired to party, didn't matter anymore. Dancing gave her a feeling of soaring, of being unique, of flying through the air when she leaped. She had been geared up for the hours of hard work, strict criticism and other things her mother had told her to be prepared for. However, she had luckily sprung further than she had hoped.

"So far, not bad, stay consistent," the choreographer told her. In the first week of shows he had corrected her a number of times and kept saying that her timing had been off in one part. But since then he hadn't complained about anything specific. She hadn't given the company reason to feel that casting her was a wrong choice. So far, her perseverance hadn't been a waste. All those hours of toiling away in Olga's studio until the sweat poured from her forehead were worth it. She remembered the days that she had pushed herself to the extreme, barely able to get up the next day with the raw pain in her body. The bleeding toes had meaning behind them. She had found it.

Night after night, she became the fairy. Playing the same part over and over didn't seem tedious in the least. At the beginning of her career, where was the need to dwell on such minor things? She had a tendency to keep whining to herself about wishing she could go higher. Nothing was ever perfect for her. She would always want something she did not have. But now, she told herself, she couldn't do that. No time for complaints, or being fussy. In fact, when the director was present, she made sure she was as respectful and nice as possible. Attitude always counted, she felt.

The show ran three times a week at the Moscow Star Ballet Theatre from 6:00 pm in the evening and there was a noon show on Saturdays. Zaria became devoted to performing every night and immersed herself in her role every single time. If she felt she hadn't done well in one show, she would mentally go over her mistakes at home, correcting, chiding, and willing herself to do better the next time. She was infatuated with performing. Every night's show was an adventure.

The *Nutcracker* ran for a month and then she was soon rehearsing for another role as the Fairy of Diamond in *Sleeping Beauty*. Another fairy role, but in one of her favourite ballets. The story was different from the Disney movie she had adored as a kid, but being in the world of fantasy and transforming into another character for the next show was an experience she hadn't had before. A different story, a different role, new costumes, new joy.

Every morning, all the dancers would do their warm up exercises and stretching in the theatre's rehearsal room. Zaria was always amongst the first to arrive, raring to go as she pulled off her T-shirt and jeans and took her place at the barres. She would hear only the director's counts as she did the barre exercises and worked her muscles hard. Everything the choreographer said, she would listen to vigilantly and follow obediently. She hoped her persistence wouldn't be buried amidst the others, but would be noticed. If providence was in a bestowing mood, maybe she would get a main part in a year or two. That would push away the qualms of being a soloist (ballerina who does secondary parts) for the rest of her life, of never being in the lead.

That spring, she got to play a friend to the Prince in the famous *Swan Lake* ballet.

She was having the time of her life. The feeling of earning her own money and being independent was something that meant so much more to her than to others. She didn't have to ask her mother for pocket money anymore, which she had done back in her college days guiltily. She was getting a monthly salary, and when she received her first pay cheque for 13,600 roubles she waved it around proudly at home, prompting Irina to berate her.

Irina didn't have to work anymore, but she continued to teach ballet twice a week because she had genuine passion for it. As a child, Zaria hadn't known the enormity of her mother's violent internal battles and sinister shadows but after she came to know a part of the tragic story, she felt acutely for her mother, whenever she thought back on those years. She knew Irina had had such a cruel life during that period, the loss of her husband never fully leaving her. Zaria was glad that her mother didn't have to support her anymore. She wanted to see her relax and the worry lines from her brow melt away. Men still gave Irina long, appreciative stares as she walked down the street, Zaria observed. They hadn't discussed it except on one occasion, but Zaria understood how her mother was trying to move on from the death of her husband. She wished that her mother would find somebody who could help her smile again, the way she used to all those years ago.

Zaria's new life left her with no time for boys. Ever since she had joined the ballet company she hadn't had the time to date anyone and this bothered her. After all, she wanted to have fun and not eat, sleep and think dance from morning to night. Since she was a ballerina, there were bound to be a lot of men lusting after her and other such pretty, young, aspiring dancers, she knew. Irina had warned her of such things, as well as told her some stories from her dancing days of unwanted attention she'd gotten from both men and women. She knew there were men who were further at the top in ballet who could lure young girls like her into sleeping with them by promising them a shortcut to stardom. But it wasn't always true. Zaria had, however, handed out sexual favours to men who mattered, something she felt just had to be done.

The next role she was assigned was in the famed Shakespearean tale *Romeo and Juliet*. She also had to understudy the role of Juliet, learning all the steps during the daily morning rehearsals. Despite the difficulty of remembering two parts, she committed all the steps to memory as best as she could. Hopefully, if the main dancer fell ill for just one day, she could step in and grab some attention.

Playing the nurse in *Romeo and Juliet*, she managed well, but she started itching for the chance to grab a main role. That was a fault Olga noticed and pointed out to her.

"If you aren't patient it may never happen. You have to learn that now or you will never do well in the present," Olga told her angrily, when Zaria visited her one morning. Olga's tone was extremely stern, and her eyes looked like she was talking to a child. She hadn't ever used that tone with her before, and it made Zaria apologise profusely and stay quiet.

The young woman knew she had to stop dreaming and be thankful for whatever she had. Main parts might not happen, and if that was where she found herself she had to accept it. Reveries couldn't turn out just the way she wanted, since she couldn't sculpt life to her taste. But, all the same, she felt she was entitled to covet that secret wish, however far-fetched, that she would dance a main role one day.

As Juliet's nurse, she kept up a consistent showing and drew more commendation from the director.

And then one day, fortune smiled on her when she least expected it, giving her the chance to climb a rung higher.

The group was touring Ukraine when the dancer playing Juliet suffered a minor hip injury. She was taken to the doctor who advised her to rest for two shows. This meant that Zaria got to take her place for those two nights. She felt the glee erupt inside her when she was told the lead was injured. The tiny amount of guilt at being happy in someone else's disappointment was there somewhere deep in her mind, but forgotten as soon as it appeared. This was her chance! The timely moment could give her a chance to prove herself.

She felt a fair amount of disquiet claw its way into her mind like never before. She had understudied the part, but had never expected to take it on so suddenly. What if she was so bad that the director yelled at her? No, no, she had to stay upbeat. She could actually do well and get her efforts noticed by the company heads. That was a remote possibility, but a real one. She could breathe life into it if the time was right. But what if it wasn't?

Chapter 10

Zaria was backstage feeling more nervous than she had ever felt before. What was wrong with her, she was never one to get fretful and tense. Normally she hardly felt any nerves when she performed, but this was no ordinary night. She chewed on one long, painted fingernail unconsciously, before she caught herself. This was a whopper of a test and she couldn't mess up this opportunity. She was the Queen tonight. A fine chance had been handed to her. It might not ever come her way again. Ever. Imagine being stuck as a soloist for the rest of her life. All those dreams of being a principal dancer (ballerina who dances the main part in a ballet) would have to be erased, forgotten or worse—might be laughed at. Not that anyone knew those secret ambitions she carried, since she kept that entirely to herself.

Soon the curtains went up and she became Juliet—the young, innocent damsel who fell in love with the son of her parents' enemy.

The emotion she had to show on her face for this part was challenging, since the character was very different from her own personality. She had a solo in the fourth scene, one that she had rehearsed in her head so many times she had lost count. She listened to the violin strains and danced as though it was just a rehearsal, letting go and enjoying the feel of the soft, brown wig she wore. Romeo fell in love with Juliet, and finally Zaria did her dramatic death scene, which the director had made her do over and over the previous day.

After the show, she had the feeling that she had done much better than she had hoped to do. She mentally congratulated herself backstage, feeling the afterglow of a satisfactory showing. She just stood awhile in the tutu that had fit her with some last minute alterations, amidst the people rushing back and forth to change. She could hear the costume mistress yelling at someone for putting a rip in one dress.

As she stood, she saw someone approaching and whipped her face around in that direction. It was the director.

"Zaria. That was very good! I didn't expect you to do so well in this role," he trailed off, giving her a pat on the back before walking away.

Zaria blinked, barely believing she had heard right. She had done well! Yes! Was she closer to landing a bigger part soon? It felt so close, almost like she could reach out and touch it, and yet it was so far away. Was she ready for it? Probably. She was already twenty two, after all. Time was short and precious.

She flew down to India to attend Gul's wedding that was happening in Chennai that December. She went to the marriage venue with one of her cousins who was also friends with the bride. Gul looked stunning in her red silk *lehenga* with crystals embroidered in intricate patterns on it. Diamond earrings adorned her ears, with more diamonds sparkling on her hands and around her neck. Gul's mother hugged countless relatives and friends who congratulated her in hordes.

Zaria greeted some friends from school who complimented her on her magenta silk sari and gold jewellery. Tara talked to her about her live-in American boyfriend in New York, where she was attending college at New York University. Her parents were as liberal about boys as Gul's were ultra-conservative. As they chatted, Farhan came up and said hello to everyone. He wore a formal maroon *sherwani* with rich gold embroidery on it.

"Hey guys! I cannot believe my little sister is getting married already," he said, beaming.

"I'm so happy for both of them," Zaria said, grinning.

The weather was pleasant and cool, a sharp contrast to the frigid winters of Moscow. Zaria said hello to her Indian friends and they all filled each other in on what they had been up to since their college days. Some mothers were already starting the process of scouting a groom for their daughters who were still in their early twenties. Zaria found the whole concept of the Indian obsession with marriage funny but cute. Gul's wedding had been arranged by her parents with a boy from another prominent Muslim family. Zaria, however, found the idea of marrying a boy picked out by her parents based on religion, community and horoscopes too bizarre to fathom. She knew her wedding would have to be a love marriage and nothing else. But would she even be able to ever fall in love? With the busy life of constant performing, it seemed nearly impossible.

The girls all walked up to Gul and gave her their good wishes and wedding gifts. Tara and Zaria had both pitched in for a pearl choker necklace for their best friend. Earlier at Gul's *mehndi* ceremony, Tara, Zaria and a few of Gul's female cousins had danced together to a Bollywood song. Zaria's friends had kidded her about doing a ballet solo but they ended up dancing to a hastily choreographed fast paced number.

Zaria glanced at the mouth watering dishes that were laid out for the guests on long tables nearby. The smell of chicken, roti and biryani was tempting, but she knew she had to be careful about what she ate.

"I can't believe we are at the marriageable age already!" Tara said suddenly, appearing next to Zaria. Zaria shook her head and smiled at her before answering.

"I really can't…We were all six years old just yesterday!"

Zaria took in how her childhood seemed to have flown by so fast. As she saw many of her school friends, some already working, some going on to master's degrees, she speculated at the direction her own life would take. She knew she didn't want the usual Indian path of marriage and a family before she was at least thirty. She was in a distinctive place, very unlike where others stood. A life of constant performing and travelling was what lay ahead of her. But the picture seemed strangely appealing.

"Hello! Look who's here!" a male voice said, shaking her out of her daydreams. Ashwin seemed to appear out of nowhere, looking smart in a blue salwar and kurta.

"Hi!" she said, giving him a long hug.

He asked how her ballet was going and how her mother was. She told him about her new show and he said he was planning to work in his family business for awhile before doing his MBA. He was still a complete cricket fanatic and even travelled around the country to watch some big matches. He mentioned that he, Devinder and Farhan were already planning to go to the next cricket World Cup.

"So some of my friends from Moscow are really curious about India and want to visit," Zaria said, picking on a bit of spicy biryani from Ashwin's plate.

"Oh yeah, tell them to drop by. And we can meet some Elenas, Igors, Viktors and Dmitrys," Ashwin said with his usual sarcastic frankness and gentle teasing.

"Shut up," she said, chortling at his repeated joke about so many Russians having the same names. Ashwin's dark brown skin looked a little less tanned and she assumed it was because he couldn't play cricket in the monsoons. His black curls were now grown to the middle of his neck. His dark eyes still had that flirtatious spark in them and his arms looked more muscular. She admitted that he was really cute, but never said it aloud because his long term crush seemed intense. She watched as he flirted with every other pretty girl, most of whom seemed to enjoy his attention. Girls thought he was hot, from what Tara and Gul had told her. But, anyway what did that have to do with anything? She was in touch with him on e-mail and they were now good friends. She came back to the chicken on her plate as she continued to chat with familiar faces, noting that she loved the sensual feel of the sari she was wrapped in. All thoughts about her future disappeared with the winds of care as the laughter of youth flowed around her.

After a year of dedicated work and performances, she was entrusted with some bigger parts. The director told her that he had thought hard and decided that she was ready for them. The moment was here. She had dreamt of dancing a main part for so long she couldn't even remember. Was she eleven or even younger when she had thought of it? Was it since she had seen a picture at home from Irina's dancing days which hung on the wall, above the dining table? She had stared at Irina dressed in a light blue tutu, lifting her leg high behind her. She looked so gorgeous, and the picture was so magnificent that Zaria had asked her grandmother to tell her more about it immediately.

The first main role she was given was in *Cinderella* and she also did the title part in *Sleeping Beauty*. Dancing these principal roles was her lifelong goal and it felt so astounding. But amidst the triumph at getting there, there was also a feeling of coming short, of emptiness. Playing princessy roles seemed to be what the directors thought she was best suited for. Those were the only parts she was given. She did her best, and the resilience to improve and prove herself grew stronger. If she wanted to take on atypical roles in the future, she knew she had to improve her dancing skills and her weaker points. For that, she needed to put in more time to work on perfecting her technique.

The next competition she took part in, she came a credible second. The winner needed no introduction. Katerina Baronova, the too famous prima ballerina.

"Congratulations," Zaria said to Katya, as she was called, after the results were announced. Katya simply threw her a look as though she was a nobody and walked away. She was twenty-six, and already had so much stardom in the media. Zaria sulked inwardly at losing out to her for the winner's slot. Why did Katya have to take part and spoil her chances of winning? Zaria felt cheated at having narrowly missed out on all the adulation. Imagine if she had won. She would have been the one in the papers, and getting all the fame. Maybe she just wasn't meant for all that this time. But second wasn't that bad, come to think of it.

One day, a choreographer called Georgio from a larger group called the Baranski Ballet was doing a workshop with the Moscow Star Ballet. He was helping all the dancers advance their skills and technique in a three day workshop. Zaria noticed Georgio watching her closely during the sessions, clearly impressed with her pirouettes and with her in general.

After the third day's workshop ended, when the others had left, Zaria stayed behind to ask Georgio for some suggestions on improving her leaps. She first thanked him and told him how helpful his workshop had been. Before she could ask him for some tips, he suddenly leaned towards her and beckoned her to come closer.

She quizzically leaned in too. Georgio placed a hand lightly on her bare shoulder, making Zaria uncomfortable.

"I have a proposal for you," Georgio whispered, his tone very quiet and secretive.

Zaria thought she hadn't heard right and said, "Um, what is it?"

"How about joining the Baranski? It is so much more prestigious. You can do well there," Georgio said, in a low voice. He stood so close that she could smell his sweat. He looked very eager and the offer sounded really enticing, dangling under her nose like precious stones.

"Wow…Well, I have to think about it," she told him. Conflict started churning inside her. She knew she mustn't make such a life-changing decision so hastily. But she changed her mind less than a second later.

"It sounds great!" she whispered, smiling.

The Baranski Theatre. It was one of the most celebrated theatres in the whole of Russia. They also toured often to places like Austria, Germany, Canada, America, Italy and England. Places Zaria could only dream of setting foot in when she was younger.

Their main director, Alexandr, was a retired ballet great who had danced with Irina on many, many occasions when they were both star dancers with the Baranski. Alexandr had been a very close friend of Irina's since those days and was very sad when she had halted her career at its peak.

"But anyway I found the whole ballet world too strenuous and liked my life in Chennai much more," Irina told Zaria.

That was the first time she had admitted to her and Zaria was completely taken aback.

Irina called and told Alexandr about her daughter's aspirations and he said that he would be more than happy to give Zaria's career a boost. Zaria auditioned in front of him and he showed an instant fondness for both her and her dancing.

"*Harasho*! Where have you been for the past few years?" he asked, his eyes peering at Zaria from under his round spectacles. When she said that she had been studying on her mother's insistence, he shook his head.

Alexandr complimented Zaria on her basic technique, which he said was quite excellent. She felt jubilant on hearing those words from someone as powerful as him. Being Irina's daughter gave her a very huge push and she was well aware of the fact. Though it wasn't the ideal way to get there, she wasn't the least bit sorry to use her mother's influence. After all, she may never win a place with the Baranski otherwise. Her pride from when she had started out had diminished somewhat. Zaria couldn't help asking her mother how

Alexandr had been so ready to give her a contract, but Irina said she would never have been picked if she wasn't good. Zaria thanked her for the reassurance but knew her ticket had been assured only due to Alexandr knowing Irina so well. She pushed that thought away and felt her felicity surge. Wow. The Baranski.

She admittedly felt a little guilty about leaving the Moscow Star Ballet, since the directors there had been the ones to discover her. Also, they had promoted her to a principal so quickly. But all this coming and going was part of life. After all, she was moving on to something more valuable. The third largest group in the country, she told herself for the hundredth time. And it had just happened to walk her way and seize her in its beckoning arms.

She was going to be dancing secondary roles once again, since the stint was mandatory for all newcomers to the Baranski. Some of her friends thought she was crazy to leave a company which was giving her principal parts, since that was what she had wanted all along.

Her personal life slowly picked up from being dreary. She met Yevgeny, a ballet patron, at a fundraiser the Baranski held very soon after she had joined the group. He was twenty-nine and was one of the most loyal patrons of the Baranski, always contributing generously at their fundraisers. Besides that, he'd inherited a fortune and was also extremely well connected in the world of ballet in Russia. Zaria did not think twice about dating him, hoping to make valuable connections for herself in the process. Having a rich boyfriend was easy with her looks, and she felt she too deserved to be pampered a bit.

Night after night of performing, hearing the claps reverberate through the theatre air, made her more determined to improve, to sparkle, to stay consistent. She and Yevgeny continued to see each other when they could, though it was possible only on weekends. She found that she was barely attracted to him at all, but anyway kept the relationship going.

Many months later came the day when things changed again.

Alexandr, the director, was watching the group rehearse one morning in the Baranski's rehearsal room. All the dancers were doing their barre exercises, following the loud, clear counts from the rehearsal director. Zaria was there as well doing the warm ups, feeling her leg muscles go taut with the stretches.

Alexandr had just announced to everyone that one of their chief dancers, Svetlana, was leaving the group. Her contract had expired and she was taking up a lucrative offer with the New York City ballet to better her prospects.

Zaria had been understudying a few of Svetlana's roles for some time, including the one of Juliet. She felt her hopes soar, then found herself forcing them down again. Why should she set herself up for a disappointment if it did not happen?

The ballet *Romeo and Juliet* was going to be staged at the Baranski after quite some time, Alexandr having just created his own version. The cast was being finalised on that day and all the dancers were very aware that someone would be stepping into Svetlana's role. Who would get it was the question on every single person's mind.

After an hour, the group had a short break to sip water and cool off. Alexandr suddenly rose from his chair and strode up to Zaria, grabbing her arm and taking her aside. She wondered why he was suddenly singling her out, even as some other dancers looked towards the two of them.

Alexandr peered at her intensely from underneath his glasses and then said, "So, my dear. Do you think you are ready for something more challenging? You have fine work ethic. Think you can take on a principal part?"

They wanted a younger face! Unbelievable. Alexandr, who had discovered some future stars, thought she was ready for a lead role! This was a moment she had waited for, had romanticised about since the day she had first joined the group. Now…it was really here.

As she walked on the roads outside, everything seemed suddenly, bright, beautiful, new. The trees were turning golden brown as autumn approached. She wanted to jump, sing even. Perhaps she should. No, she couldn't get overconfident. But it had happened. To her. At the Baranski Ballet.

Chapter 11

Rehearsals began daily, in the mornings and Zaria ensured she was always there ahead of time. The theatre's rehearsal room was huge, with a dull brown wooden floor and mirrors lining one wall. Low benches stood in front of the mirrors. Light streamed in from the glass windows and a long tube light along one wall cast a pale white light over the dancers. All the dancers always began with the warm up and bar exercises before proceeding to their parts for the shows. Alexandr sat on a bench, his eyes watching the rehearsal carefully from behind his round spectacles. Being the chief director and choreographer, he was almost always present. This version of *Romeo and Juliet* was his latest creation, something with his own newly choreographed steps.

Zaria was rehearsing her solo as Juliet, and made sure she followed the choreographer's instructions down to the minutest detail. Some dancers were standing at the other end of the room, learning their parts. The rehearsal supervisor stood near Alexandr, holding a clipboard and pen.

Zaria moved lightly on the floor, her pointe shoes barely making a sound. She counted mentally as she twirled, trying to get the rhythm correct. She could glimpse her slender form in the mirrors, wrapped tightly in her new leotard. It felt a little too tight, but she was more worried about what the director thought now. When she finished, she looked at the assistant choreographer who stood a few feet away. The skinny, red haired man demonstrated another sequence of steps which she observed meticulously.

"You need to have a very delicate feel, remember," he said, in rapid Russian.

Zaria did the same steps, the floor cool under her shoes. Jete, pirouette, ballonne, stay light, look happy. The higher standard of dancing expected of her was not easy to adjust to right away.

"That was very good, my dear. But you have to look more innocent," Alexandr's voice rang out with his thick Russian accent as soon as she finished, making her inhale sharply. She stood straight and looked at him obediently, nodding her head without saying a word.

Alexandr seemed happy with her dancing so far. Zaria knew he was one of the most celebrated choreographers in the world, who had been the head of the Baranski for the past three years. Most of the ballets here were versions created by him. Alexandr was also gay, Zaria knew from her mother. His face was rounded with a thick nose, thin lips and a kindly expression. Curly grey hair grew behind a balding hairline, only a few strands of brown visible. He was clearly overweight since his retirement from dancing. Overall, he gave the impression of a sweet, paunchy teddy bear.

The assistant choreographer spoke too fast and she had to struggle to catch every word.

"In the allegro tut, more energy. And your arm must be here," he said, twirling with his arm above his head.

He was very blunt when she did a step wrong and rarely commended her. Zaria took down notes in her notebook, writing down specific steps in the exact words that he and Alexandr instructed her in.

"Good you're writing it down, remember to mention lifting that leg higher on the assemble," Alexandr said.

Alexandr was clearly partial to her, which Zaria felt was because she was Irina's daughter. She was certain that some other dancers resented it when Alexandr complimented her or said 'well done' to her dancing. During rehearsal breaks, she wiped her sweat with a towel and sat down on the benches, trying not to speak too much. Alexandr's rules during rehearsals were strict—no talking or text messaging except during breaks. She could feel the kind of unspoken jealousy in the air between her and another girl called Maria, who had lost out to her on her part. From the few awkward monosyllabic conversations they had had during rehearsals, Zaria knew that Maria was two years younger than her. But she mostly ignored the envious looks that Maria threw at her. Maria looked like she was hoping Zaria would fracture her ankle. Zaria too had felt the same way not too long ago, when she was an understudy.

She was able to pick up steps without much difficulty, having always been a quick learner. Some of the other dancers were nice enough to her and she felt comfortable in her new role within a few weeks. During lunch breaks, she ate at the theatre's canteen on the lunch vouchers the dancers were given. She usually sat with two of her new friends—Igor and Victor. They had both danced with the Baranski for nearly five years and were happy to share their experiences with her. Igor, who played Tybalt, was a guy Zaria got along with really well. He was three years older than her and openly gay. Zaria had never had a problem with gay guys and in fact, was very happy being friends with them. Igor was tall with longish, dark brown hair and a stubble on his chin. His jokes during the rehearsal breaks had the rest of the dancers in splits.

"So Alexandr is a much nicer director than the last one. The other one was too strict and his wife was such a problem when she watched rehearsals. Her face had a stiff frown permanently stuck on and her voice sounded like an angry baboon's," Igor said, making Zaria giggle.

"And, I should tell you about the most fun tour we had to Italy, Milan…" Victor said. Zaria turned towards him, seated next to her, on the other side at the table. Victor was a year younger than her and looked like a schoolboy with his lean build and short black hair. He was gay too and much quieter than Igor.

"Wow, Milan! What was that like?" Zaria asked, her voice rising in excitement.

"Awesome. The sightseeing, the food, the gorgeous guys…Some of the girls got their butts pinched and we felt we had to guard them, though they didn't mind the pinches," Victor joked. "We all wanted to sneak off to explore the city more."

"And remember the day I hid that rubber frog in Dina's bag and how loudly she screamed?" Igor reminisced, gesturing with his fork, his eyes looking mischievous.

Zaria laughed with them, amused at their anecdotes. She picked up some carrots and pasta from her plate with a fork. The food tasted much better than the fare at her old theatre. Everything seemed bigger and better.

The coach assigned to Zaria for her special classes for the main role was Vanya, a sixty-year-old former ballet star. Vanya had enjoyed a stellar career during the Soviet era and remained amongst the greatest legends in Russian ballet. She was of stocky build and had straight, grey hair which grew to her neck. The lines on her face were barely noticeable and as she sat on the bench her posture showed refinement.

Vanya rehearsed Zaria, and instructed her as she did a part of her routine.

"You can perfect your jetes with more practice. Your pirouettes are good but you need more flexibility in your leg lifts," Vanya said, her voice regal and deep.

Zaria practised and repeated the parts she was told to, carefully listening to her coach's criticism. She could hear only Vanya's instructions and the soft hum of the heater, a warm contrast to the nippy air outside. Vanya was considerably stricter with her than Olga had been, telling Zaria her weaknesses bluntly.

Zaria remembered Olga's teaching methods clearly and often felt emotional at leaving the woman who had nurtured her talent. Olga had after all been the one who had brought her where she was. But they were still in touch and stayed close.

Zaria soon found that Vanya's teaching was exactly what she needed, at a stage where her sudden breakthrough had made her slightly overconfident. After she practised her leaps and splits, Vanya smiled at her in appreciation.

"Your technique is basically strong. And you have confidence and discipline which I like in dancers," she said, her eyes firm.

Zaria felt pleased at the compliment and told Vanya that she would work hard on all her weak points. She asked if she could do some extra homework or sessions specifically to better her leaps. She had very little stage experience compared to the dancer in the male lead. Romeo was being played by a twenty-seven-year-old Italian dancer called Vincenzo who had danced numerous main parts for many years in France before moving to the Baranski a few months ago. He looked extremely handsome with his longish dark brown hair, deep black eyes and chiselled features.

Zaria and Vincenzo had to rehearse the very important duet many times to get their coordination and timing right. The pianist played on the grand piano on the far right, the notes from the haunting melody rising harmoniously. The two dancers danced to the tune, listening and moving.

"More sensuality, it has to look very intimate," Alexandr called out after Vincenzo lifted Zaria slowly and set her down again.

The translator had to translate what was said for Vincenzo, who spoke only a few words of Russian. Zaria could barely communicate with him, but they had to ensure that they were well coordinated. Fortunately, they were able to dance well together, despite the language problem. She developed a big crush on Vincenzo and felt it when she danced very close to him. His body was really muscular and she couldn't stop admiring it. Whenever he put his arms on her back, around her waist or lifted her, she was very conscious of his touch and felt light-headed. She made a mental note to tell her friends later, they would find it hilarious. Her crush was harmless, something she poked fun at herself for. On stage, she had to act as if she was in love with Vincenzo anyway, and putting on a lovestruck expression wouldn't be a problem at all. Vincenzo spoke very little, and anyway, she didn't want to get involved with another dancer since dancers at the Baranski were not allowed to date.

"Zaria, a little slower when you bend back," Alexandr said after they danced a section of the duet again.

"Sorry, sir. I'll remember that," she said, making a mental note.

"Both of you have good chemistry and good coordination, keep that up!" Alexandr said, waving his hands like an opera conductor.

After two hours, Alexandr said, 'Well done!', and clapped, almost beaming, his pleasure obvious.

He then made them rehearse the death scene at the end of the ballet countless times, correcting them as he stood in front, observing every detail. Sweat clung to Zaria's leotard, brow and hair, but she was barely conscious of the stickiness or smell. Juliet's death scene was an arduous and challenging one for her. She had to portray a range of emotions in the scene. After trying to wake Romeo up, she had to portray her hysteria at his death, kill herself in her grief and then lie absolutely still and remain limp playing dead. She had never done a dramatic death scene before, except for those two days when the lead at Moscow Star Ballet was out of commission with a minor hip injury. The scene had not been taught to her in such detail before. So the concept was something new, more so given Alexandr's intense choreography. The music for the scene had a sad, dark tone. She tried to get into the sound completely, letting her body feel and express the sorrow.

"Dance with more anguish when you realise your love is dead. More!" Alexandr said, as she tried harder and harder to get the scene right. She tried to imagine a reason that would make her understand the monstrous pain Juliet felt at losing her young husband. She pictured herself failing to become a ballerina and never being able to accept that for the rest of her life. Or, she could think of her mother when she was widowed.

She had to stab herself in the stomach with a sword, crawl slowly onto a flat, grey surface and then die. She found this part much more difficult than the previous bit, especially the stabbing part. She knew the fake sword went into itself and wouldn't hurt her, but still plunged it into herself tentatively at first, getting a firm grip on the thick handle and getting used to the movement.

"Good, but faster—like this, my dear," Alexandr said, walking up to her and taking the sword from her hand. He then proceeded to thrust it swiftly into his huge, flabby stomach for fun, even giving Zaria a smile of encouragement. She simply nodded as he handed the sword back to her. Alexandr then strode over to Vincenzo and described certain corrections he had to make in the scene. Zaria breathed deeply, in and out, running her part over in her mind, trying to visualise herself doing it perfectly.

When the show was two weeks away, they got to rehearse on the theatre's main stage a few times. The stage was massive and as Zaria danced on it, she felt her love for ballet flow through every particle in her being. It was visible in every part of the stage, every step she took. The music from the orchestra gave her a lift as she danced. The very air on the stage seemed holy, something that she couldn't believe she was worthy of breathing.

The famous Baranski Theatre had an aura of greatness. The ceiling had a bronzed gold colour with patterns carved on the sides. In the middle of the ceiling were figures from Russian mythology. Balcony seats were on either side of the stage, with deep red curtains running along the top. The fronts of the balconies were golden and engraved with intricate patterns—spirals, figures and symmetrical designs. They looked grand, even royal. A deep red carpet ran in the centre between the plush maroon seats. As she had walked in, Zaria had lifted her eyes up and taken in all the corners of the room, marvelling as she climbed up to the stage. The hall looked majestic in its quiet stillness. Looking out at the rows of empty seats in the auditorium, Zaria imagined faces filling them. Old and young, oval and round, they would be watching her. VIPs would sit in the balcony in their silks, with their opera glasses.

Later, she sat down while some dancers rehearsed the scene where Tybalt killed Mercutio. Igor made an immense show of his duel scene, flourishing his sword and stabbing it with extra gusto, prompting Alexandr to berate him for fooling around. Zaria sat watching in the front row, a few chairs away from the crew. Here was a point in her life where she could use the chance and climb further up the ladder, to a higher step. The opportunity may never come her way again. She felt an overpowering resolution to perfect her role for the opening night. A very solid breakthrough had happened and she needed that luck to remain with her throughout the performance. For the time being, the fact that Alexandr liked her dancing abilities, and had taken the risk of casting her, was fantastic. She had been glad to hear that her youth and beauty had helped her in securing the part.

Was it really here, the moment she had been waiting for, for so many years? The upcoming show would be the most colossal moment in her career. Perhaps she was making too big a deal of it, but she couldn't help feeling that eager thrill inside.

As the premiere drew nearer she started a countdown. When she forgot a little step or felt a twinge in her left foot, she had a brief flash of anxiety. Her nervousness was otherwise nowhere as much as her sheer excitement. At home, her mood was so good it surprised her mother. Irina said that her grin was so wide her mouth might get stuck that way. The dress rehearsals came and went, with more corrections to her solo. Zaria's anticipation mounted as the premiere came even closer. She had never felt such a drive to dance outstandingly ever before. The audience had to be wowed.

Chapter 12

The dressing room had walls in pastel shades and a large mirrored dressing table. Makeup boxes with tubes and brushes stood open on one side of the dressing table. A makeup artist touched up Zaria's face with blush and lipstick, as she watched her reflection in the mirror. The brush tickled her lightly as it made her cheeks pinker and rosier.

A tall cupboard stood against the left wall with her spare costume and the other costumes she needed for the show. A huge clock, gold and green with a Russian historical figure painted onto it hung above the mirror. Zaria thought the room had a historic beauty to it. This was where so many famous ballerinas had sat before they performed their major roles. She wasn't the only person performing in her biggest show yet. Another girl was too, but she was nineteen and Zaria had felt jealous when she watched her perform so well during rehearsals. Not that she felt she herself wasn't good enough. She was here, after all.

She glanced at the clock, at the gold hands on it and the seconds ticking. It read 6:45 pm. Only a little time left before her debut as Juliet. The barely audible tick was rhythmic, counting down faster than she wanted it to. She came to with a start, realising she had let her thoughts wander too long. Listening to some music usually helped her relax when she was tense, but she hadn't brought her iPod with her. This was the biggest day of her life. If she made a mistake after so much rehearsing, she knew she would be totally devastated. She wanted so badly to perform well, but the thought of not doing that almost scared her. Terrifying, but no point in getting paranoid. She picked up her little black cell phone from her purse and checked her messages. Her mother had sent her a text message just about half an hour ago. It read—

Sweetheart, remember to pray just before you go on. It's important. Good luck.

Irina was seated in the audience. Galya hadn't been able to come since she had trouble walking with her knee problem. Zaria was grateful for her mother's guidance, though she had only advised her about which groups to try out for and where to start. She didn't tell her what to do in the dance world, unless Zaria asked. The young woman wanted the space to make her own mistakes when she was just starting out and her mother had given her that space.

She said her prayers and then glanced at her makeup in the mirror one last time. She had sat for nearly two hours getting ready, and had touched up her lipstick so many times she was feeling obsessive. Her fake eyelashes made her look sultry, even if she thought so herself. She couldn't help admiring her face with the thick foundation, smoky light blue eye shadow and light lipstick. She had the young, girlish look that Juliet had to have. Slipping into the silky, pale pink tulle dress with its pearly design made her feel sexy, the costume accentuating her slim figure and her small waist. Her hair was dyed darker brown, and curled slightly at the ends. She looked both feminine and sensuous, just the right blend needed.

She glanced again at the small ruled notebook that lay open on her lap, in which she had scrawled pointers to herself during rehearsals. *Death scene, keep face anguished. Duet, show tenderness, innocence, light on feet…*

She closed the book. No need to look at the notes now, they were suddenly confusing. The pre-show nerves and anxiety her mother had warned her about were there, lying dormant behind the hope and desire to impress that showed in her sea green eyes. Her heart was still full of ambition. Perhaps she could excel and get accolades for it. All those days and weeks of practice had to show today.

She reached into her bag and took out the recently broken in pair of ballet shoes she was to wear for that evening. They were silvery, made of satin, which matched her silver coloured silk stockings, new ones that she was wearing for the first time since the fittings. The colour went with her pale outfit and makeup perfectly, giving her a dash of softness. Walking to the wings of the stage, she did the usual stretches for her muscles, trying to get her body ready. She kept running through her part in her mind, unable to relax or even stop worrying about forgetting something when she was on stage.

The curtains rose. She could hear the sounds of the classical composition faintly. She entered the large room near the wings, where most of the other dancers were waiting. Two other ballerinas who were dancing minor roles waited on the couch on the opposite end of the room. They all barely spoke to each other. Zaria watched girls much younger than her and couldn't help feeling that it could have been her two, even three years earlier, on the threshold of breaking through. She glanced around the room, at the dancers in their skin-tight costumes, some talking on their cell phones, others going over the steps trying to pass the time. Some were stretching on the bars that were against a wall. The sounds of the stagehands in charge of the props frantically calling out to each other about what to move when was mixed into the pre-show tension in the air.

The dresser was yelling at some girl in the corps, who seemed to be in a frenzy about her costume being too tight.

"Don't worry. It won't tear," she said, looking exasperated even as the girl whined some more.

The backstage hysteria that Alexandr was exhibiting was the most hilarious.

"Why was that prop touched up only this morning? I said it had to be ready two days ago!" he shouted at the stage manager. His hands gestured wildly as he continued to rant in rapid Russian. He then called two of the dancers who were sitting down and gave them last minute instructions. Zaria had to smile at his nervousness. They all felt it, but she just didn't show it as much as the others.

She had gone over the steps enough number of times, she probably knew them backwards. Besides the rehearsals that they all worked at until their limbs burned, she had run through her routines at home when she had nothing else to do.

The show began, the opening set in the streets of Verona in Italy. Vincenzo was on stage playing Romeo, she knew, since she could hear the music waft over to where she was. She went on only in the Second Act, when Juliet was in her room. The First Act seemed to fly by and she was soon on stage as Juliet. She slipped into the role, as the light shone down on her, playing the innocent, teenaged damsel. Juliet's mother came in to tell her that she had to be married. So far, she hadn't forgotten anything.

Then there was the scene of the ball at the Capulets, where she felt her tension build up with every passing second. She had a solo dance here and had to do it well. She entered the scene from the door at the back. The sets had been changed to show a party scene. All the guests were dancing around her. She had to slip into the character of Juliet, amidst all the others around the stage, in their black and green and gold costumes dancing together. As she danced, she knew it was the oxygen she needed to live. This was what she was living for—to fly through the air when she leapt. To be a performer.

She began a close, slow dance with Igor first, holding onto him tightly as he lifted her. Both of them moved together, hands touching, but she was never uncomfortable dancing with her friend. Then she started her solo, the dance that would make Romeo watch entranced and fall in love with Juliet. The spotlight was trained on her, the circle of light covering her as she moved. As she kept dancing, the feeling of being on stage overwhelmed her and she soon forgot there were thousands of people watching her. She could feel the gracefulness flow through her, as she felt her costume rustle against her body softly. The score from the orchestra seemed to fill the huge stage and the large theatre, as she danced. The music filled her with an ease, a feeling of comfort she would never experience anywhere else.

She looked out into the audience. The crowd seemed so much larger here, than at the Moscow Star Ballet Theatre. She could see the grand balcony of the theatre, the golden ones. In the distance was the box where the super important people sat. So large. Everyone was watching, today was the premiere.

She was born for the stage. It was the place where she truly belonged, part of the life she had always wanted. Here she was—living it, breathing it, performing. She coasted through the air. That magical feeling of awe, of grandness, as she danced amidst the stage sets of Verona exhilarated her. There was nothing like the spotlight and the sense of independence and freedom she felt as she performed. Her teachers had always told her that her elegant style was her strong point. Adrenaline coursed through her veins, making her feel truly alive. She felt her legs and ankles stretch, the muscles in them move familiarly. The score flowed into her, making her dance with energy and power. She felt the magic of a live show clearly and knew she belonged in this world. The theatre was cold, even with the heating, but she felt the lights from above shine down on her, making her sweat as she continued. Then Romeo declared his love for her. She pulled the mask from his face, revealing a handsome young man. She had to act like she was struck by his good looks, something that was easy since Vincenzo looked gorgeous in his makeup. And then there was the balcony scene, where she acted as though in a trance, dreaming of Romeo, even when she knew he was the son of her father's enemy. As Vincenzo and she danced closely in an intimate duet, she felt almost giddy, when he lifted her and held her close. They danced, and she acted like she was very much in love. They became Shakespeare's famous lovers.

Then came the tragic ending. Juliet woke up from her sleep and saw that Romeo was really dead. Zaria had to move from this side to that, going mad with the pain of losing him. Her young heart broke as her planned elopement had gone terribly wrong. She fell to the ground, stabbing herself with the sword. And then she had to stay still, playing dead, as Romeo woke up, and raged with grief. Vincenzo had to drag her on the ground in this scene, and she tried not to make a sound, as he did so, pulling her by the hair across the wooden floor. Ouch. How she wished this scene could have been choreographed differently. She didn't manage it as well as she had hoped, but it was her best effort.

Vincenzo gave her a long kiss. She felt herself tingle as he kissed her. She listened to the music, and then she waited until Romeo had finished his dramatic death scene. As she lay still, like Juliet dead of tragic love, the sweat glistened off her face and neck, and small beads of perspiration flowed down her skin. She heard the last scene end, and the crowd's applause. What a noise!

She raised herself off the table she had been lying on, and took her bow with Vincenzo. She had done it! Many were giving them a standing ovation. So many looked like tourists, but there seemed to be many Muscovites too. But wow! So many of them. The number of seats filled looked so vast suddenly, boundless. She beamed, as the claps seemed to echo within the theatre, bouncing off the tall walls and ceiling, and flowing on to the stage. A bouquet of flowers was handed to her and she accepted it, standing tall and poised.

In the dressing room backstage, she peeled her costume off quickly and handed it to the costume mistress. After she changed and wrapped a scarf around her neck, she looked at herself in the mirror. The makeup was still on her face, though she had tried to remove some of it. She headed out the back door to meet her mother who crushed her in a large hug. Yevgeny was out of town on an important meeting and had been unable to come.

The two women drove off to a celebratory dinner. Outside the sky was dark, but the stars seemed to fill them, each brighter than the other, when Zaria glanced overhead. The adrenaline from the show still filled her, making her more energetic than tired. She knew she wouldn't be able to sleep that night, at least not for a long time.

Chapter 13

She whistled as she stretched idly with her feet up on the brown couch by the window. The seat sank in around her as she lay back and rested her head on the squashy, soft leather headrest. Her rent-free, cosy, new flat was one of the privileges she was entitled to as a principal with the Baranski. A television set with a new DVD player below it stood on a wooden shelf case, propped against the wall across. A small, square wooden table sat on the carpet in front of her couch. Thick curtains hung on either side of the tall glass windows to the right that looked out onto the street. Zaria could hear the sound of vehicles going by faintly, since the flat was situated in a quiet neighbourhood.

She adored her new place which boasted a roomy bedroom and the homely sitting room she was currently in. The air freshener she had sprayed lent a flowery fragrance to the room, new and stimulating, like everything in the flat. She got up and sauntered over to the kitchen with her feet naturally a little turned out, a ballerina's gait. The floor was cool under her bare feet, feet which were nowhere as pretty as the rest of her. Her toes were ugly and misshapen from ballet, many nails broken from standing on point. Opening the fridge door, she pulled out a bottle of milk that stood ready near the can of energy drink on the inside shelf. She skimmed her eyes fleetingly over the contents of the fridge. Hmm. She needed to buy more eggs as well as some fish. She had a food allowance too, so no expenses were incurred in that area either. The dustbin near the fridge contained some cigarettes, besides the other garbage she had thrown in there. She liked smoking and kept at it to stay thin.

She opened the wooden cupboard above the microwave and took out a white, porcelain bowl and tablespoon. Then she pulled out a large packet of cereal, pouring herself a generous helping. The crunchy corn flakes and warm milk was her first meal of the day in her strict diet plan. When she finished the bowl, she poured herself a second, smaller helping.

Suddenly, it dawned on her what day it was. She dropped her spoon, jumped up and rushed to her mailbox near the front door. When she saw that the monthly issue of *Ballet* magazine had arrived, her heart pounded faster. She grabbed the issue, covered in plastic, from the mailbox. The soft, glossy magazine was the chief news on the current ballet scene in Russia and around the world. Zaria cringed at the picture of the blonde ballerina with too much eye makeup on the cover. Katya of course. Bold font below the picture read, 'EXCLUSIVE INTERVIEW WITH KATYA—THE INTERNATIONAL SUPERSTAR!'

She quickly flipped the magazine open and searched through the index, finding the page number she wanted and urgently turning to it.

The middle section of the magazine carried a steady feature on rising ballet stars. Zaria saw her name on the first page of the article, along with the names of the two others being profiled. She sat down on the couch clutching the magazine and looked at her full-length picture, breaking into a satisfied grin. She looked really photogenic.

The photographer had captured her leaning against a cupboard in a short, low-neck dress, pouting seductively at the camera. She had spent a fortune on the dress, but the point was everyone who was anyone in the ballet world read this publication and would see it. The picture made her look both wholesome and sexy, just the blend she wanted. The deep green dress enhanced her green eyes and showed off her long legs too. The interview was printed on the right side of her portrait and covered two whole pages, which gave her the much needed publicity. She scanned through the interview, feeling a tingle of disbelief as she read her own words in print.

So tell us how your journey with ballet first began.

Well, my mother Irina was a ballerina herself and she encouraged me to follow my ambitions. I took my classes at Olga's academy very seriously and dreamed of being a professional ballerina.

You are now being touted as one of the rising stars to watch, after your fantastic run playing Juliet with the Baranski. How does the success feel?

Well, thank you. Success, honestly, isn't something I expected to taste so soon but it feels fantastic. It's flattering to be called a rising star and I hope to live up to the label. I also want to take on more varying roles in the future.

Zaria read that bit and remembered having to bite back, "I so wish I wasn't stuck with doing princessy roles right from the start."

You mentioned you had your early training at Olga's renowned academy right here in Moscow .

Yes. Olga is such a wonderful person and the most fantastic teacher I could ever ask for. I am where I am today because of her. I am still close to her and can call her for advice.

What is being a part of the Baranski like? And how is it working with Alexandr?

Oh, everyone at the Baranski is so nice and welcoming. Alexandr is such an accomplished director and we all respect him so much. I feel so fortunate that he picked me to take on the role of Juliet. He is an amazing person.

Zaria smiled as she read on, knowing it was obvious that she sounded eager to please those who mattered. She'd been honest about a bad review giving her a sleepless night occasionally.

Her Indian background and South Indian father had generated a large amount of interest and questions. She had spoken about his sudden death and how Irina and she had to go through a period of great grief before getting used to life without him. The interviewer had asked her about her Jewish and Hindu spiritual beliefs too. As she read on, she thought she had done pretty well for a first interview, sounding intelligent and honest.

"My philosophy in life is to wake up and enjoy each day as it comes."

Zaria didn't call her friends and tell them she was in the magazine, though she was intoxicated with her current success. She was going to be receiving an award the next month as one of the 'Rising stars of the year' from the Russian Ballet Council in Moscow. The award was bestowed upon new talent who were part of Russian ballet companies. Zaria was also delighted to see her name on the Baranski website with her picture, bio and repertoire on the list of twelve principal dancers.

Her life hadn't actually changed that much after being contracted as a principal dancer though she appreciated her new perks. The Baranski had given her a rent-free flat and more money besides convenient transportation to and from rehearsals. She was also entitled to a generous ballet shoe allowance of over two dozen pairs a month, a long way from the times she had to save for months to buy just one pair. But despite a better lifestyle, she remained the same person she had always been. She still had the same set of friends though she rarely had days off and thus had very few chances to hang out with them. Her days were a hectic maze of rehearsals and shows that resembled the life of a professional athlete. Evenings were the shows and mornings were the rehearsals for the next show. This was a daily routine, with just a few hours gap between rehearsals and starting makeup for the evening. Weekends were a little more leisurely. She performed one show on Saturday afternoons and so had those evenings off. The theatre also had no shows on Sunday. Those mornings, Zaria usually loved to go to Friendship Park, where she just lazed around on the grass and listened to her iPod. She also liked to take in the occasional opera concert at the Baranski, for which she got free tickets. Some weekends she had to go to the beauty parlour to get facials, pedicures and every other beauty regimen done. She had never liked going to parlours much, but now had to ensure that she looked elegant and chic every single day. She loved her body and started to look after it with much more sensitivity. Her relationship with it was now much more intimate than years before. She had to ensure she kept it healthy and didn't abuse it with drugs or overexertion. The worry every dancer had when they got cramps was not alien to her either and she was careful with every part of her body. She got a massage from the Baranski's masseuse a few times a week and massaged certain muscles with ointments after every show.

But those who saw her on stage could only see the glamorous façade of her life, the performing. They couldn't see all the clay needed to meld that behind the scenes—the long hours of slogging away and perfecting steps every day, the injuries and the exhaustion. After most shows she would find herself too tired to go out and would just flop on her bed and fall asleep instantly. Sometimes the adrenaline after a riveting performance kept her awake in bed for hours, making her quietly dream of her profile growing—of captivating audiences around the world, winning competitions, rising to superstardom.

The ballet world was looking her way and taking notice of her, and she was aware of that. She wanted to hold their gaze and give them more to talk about. Her mother's contacts weren't the only reasons for her landing where she was. If she hadn't proved herself in the talent pool, she knew she wouldn't be with such a famous theatre. But her newfound status as a principal dancer made her feel reborn. The lure of greater heights seemed to beckon her from high up, like a blaze of glory she was longing for, and would do almost anything to reach.

Her new life as a principal ballerina with the Baranski meant that she received invitations to a range of glitzy events—movie premieres, fashion shows and wine and cheese dos. When she could rarely spend an evening out at these kind of places, she felt she was now part of high society. And she had earned it. But the nights that she went out were now rare, unlike years before. The new life she was living was mostly work and little time to play.

She attended the opening of a high end designer boutique one evening, a ritzy Page Three affair. She strode into the room confidently in a knee-length sleeveless black dress, stiletto heels and long earrings. She was a *somebody* now, having been featured in *Vogue* just the previous week. And she certainly felt the confidence as she stood on the polished marble floor. She looked around and spotted several celebrities—some actors, actresses, heiresses and high-flying socialites who were Page Three regulars. The boutique was very large with smooth, lavish interiors. Racks of designer clothes stood all around, and some women were exclaiming at the dresses they liked. Zaria blended in well, and didn't feel out of place in the least.

A waiter came towards her with a tray laden with drinks. She picked up a glass of champagne that was probably worth more than six thousand roubles and sipped it, savouring the taste. The thin, cool stem of the glass seemed to fit perfectly into her fingers, as she walked over to where more people stood. Different clusters of people congregated in various areas and she could hear people conversing—some formally, some familiarly. Zaria had a special VIP invite when she stepped in and was soon introduced by the host, a middle aged woman with dyed red hair, a dress that must have cost a fortune and oodles of tiny diamonds on her necklace.

"May I present Zaria Krishnan, a principal dancer with the famous Baranski," the woman said with a flourish of her hands, as though Zaria was a prize she was keen to show off.

The people standing around looked at Zaria with intrigue and said things like, “Oh, wow”, “I love their ballets. Which one are you dancing in now?”

“Thank you so much. I’m currently dancing in *Romeo and Juliet,*” Zaria said, beaming at everyone. All of them were part of the elite cream of the city, and they were actually paying attention to her!

“Thank you so much for the invitation, Mrs Dubkova. Your boutique looks great,” she said to the host.

“You’re welcome, dear. And call me Vera, please,” the woman said, smiling and patting Zaria on her shoulder.

Being treated like an important guest and creating a flutter gave Zaria a feeling of pride. An aura was forming around her. She smiled and chatted effortlessly, like she was born to do just that. She knew she looked classy and was able to mingle with everyone while a few celebrity photographers worked the room. Being a social butterfly had always been something she was a natural at. More than one man came over to her to say hello and introduce himself. She thoroughly enjoyed their attention and flirtations, fully aware that her beauty and the allure of being a ballerina were the reasons.

Just then she noticed a strikingly beautiful blonde woman who strode into the boutique with the sound of high heels. People turned to look at her, whispering about her in awe. She was tall and slender, with green cat-like eyes and her light, sleek blonde hair was swept into a bun with an expensive looking jewelled hairclip. She had high, sculpted cheekbones and wore deep magenta lipstick. Diamonds hung from both her ears. Zaria recognised her as the most famous of all the ballerinas in Russia. Katerina Baronova, or Katya as she was called, was one of the biggest celebrities in the country, being steadily featured in a stream of magazines and TV spots over the years. She was a star dancer with the Balshoy Theatre, the biggest and most exalted ballet company in the country, and in the world. If that wasn’t enough, Katya also got rave reviews from critics for all her shows. Other ballerinas disliked Katya because she just had too much success for anyone to stomach.

Katya wasn't just a ballet legend—she was also dripping in cash. She had been married first at eighteen to a millionaire and then at twenty-two to the then director of the Balshoy, something dancers loved alluding to as the reason for her rapid rise since. She had been the youngest principal dancer in Russia at age eighteen and was a graduate of the Balshoy Academy ballet school where she had studied since age ten.

Zaria watched the effect Katya had on her audience—people turned around to look at her, whispering and pointing discreetly. She flashed a smile and kissed the hostess on both cheeks as the photographers clicked away furiously. Zaria envied Katya more than anyone else. She secretly hoped to be as famous as her one day. Right then, she was bursting with curiosity to talk to her just once. After a minute, she tentatively stepped up to the group where she stood. Katya was holding court amidst a group of admirers, mostly men who were drooling on her every word.

They turned when Zaria walked up to them and Katya's eyebrows shot up.

"Hi Katya. By the way, the Balshoy's *Don Quixote* you danced in was mindblowing. I saw it just last week," Zaria began.

"Fine. And by the way, who are you?" Katya asked, looking at her as though she was a fly.

"Oh I'm Zaria Krishnan. I am a dancer with the Baranski," Zaria said, trying to smile.

"Ahh yes. I hear Alexandr dear just adores you. Anyway…" she said, as she signed an autograph for a man who held a paper and pen out eagerly. "I must warn you dear, the ballet world is really fickle. You are the favourite one minute and the next you can be nobody… Oh, Tatiana!" she exclaimed, breaking off and rushing to a woman whom she spotted some distance away.

Zaria awkwardly excused herself from the group and walked away. What a diva. She was trying to make conversation but Katya was barely even acknowledging her. She felt resentment and jealousy boil inside her instantly as she glanced Katya's way. Her face looked so fake and plastic, the way she was laughing at someone's joke. The neckline of her gold dress was a bit too low, revealing half her breasts. Zaria's face assumed a smug expression as she took a sip from the tiny glass of champagne she was holding. It suddenly tasted a little too bitter as she swallowed it.

The attention she received from men since she had become a ballerina was more and more evident with each passing day. She received red roses and exotic bouquets from admirers quite often backstage in her dressing room. She was fond of getting the bouquets, inhaling the sweet scent of the long stemmed roses and keeping some in her apartment. She loved to read the handwritten notes that were attached to some, things like 'I loved watching you dance. You are a goddess.' Some were so bold as to say that they would fantasise about her naked body after watching the way it moved.

She found all this flattering and she wasn't complaining at all. A number of her rose-sending devotees said in the notes that they had seen her dance, very many times. She didn't know the faces behind the bouquets. But it was great to know she was wanted. Having fans felt like more support behind her. When she had looked up the names that were scrawled on some cards, she found some to be millionaires from the city, some even billionaires. The fact was exciting, but she didn't want to think about men now. Her sole focus was her dancing. She didn't have time for anything else.

She hadn't really had the time for a relationship for more than a year since her last man had found her too busy. For the time being, she was content with just having one night stands with men she found desirable. Right now, she wanted to just immerse herself in ballet and get better and better, until she felt she couldn't improve any more. She was also dying to travel the world on tours and see all the exotic places she had dreamt of.

In India, from what her friends had told her, her story had generated a lot of buzz, especially within the family. The thought gave her some solace, as people in India never initially understood her dancing ambitions, much to her chagrin. Some had stared at her like she was an alien when she said she wasn't doing a full four year degree at a university and just wanted to dance. Society in India didn't respect artists at all, unless they made money. This fact was something she found to be extremely sad in a country so rich in culture. But her cousins and close friends had always been really encouraging, knowing her heart had always been with ballet.

She wasn't feeling the need to do things like modelling to be more glamorous, though she had been asked. Katya had modelled and even done some acting but Zaria wasn't interested in fame at all now strangely. She had done a lipstick advertisement for a magazine a year ago because she needed some publicity at the time. Now she preferred to let her dancing speak for itself. Not that work was on her mind from morning to night. She woke up and thought that every day was a beautiful one, a day full of things to enjoy and laugh about. When she had holidays in winter and summer, she wanted to just unwind with family and friends and not think or speak about ballet.

Yet she was always alert, not wanting to lose her footing and decelerate in her career. The discipline and work ethic she was complimented on remained firmly ingrained in her, along with her happy-go-lucky attitude.

Chapter 14

She came down with a bad case of the flu in the middle of November, when outside temperatures dipped to below minus twenty degrees. Outside, the cold was so ferocious that it seeped into her nose and skin despite sweaters, prompting her to fall ill. She was forced to miss three shows on the doctor's advice. Being unable to dance for those three nights made her feel immensely aggravated, like an ugly monster she couldn't slay was blocking her path. She cursed aloud while stuck in her room and threw a pillow across the floor. What if the understudy shone on stage and what if the director thought she was better? No, he couldn't think that. The part belonged to her after all, and she had performed it for so many nights. She had played her part well and was more talented than the understudy. Just three days. It wasn't a big deal. They would be over in a jiffy.

They were soon gone and she was back on stage. She thoroughly enjoyed performing night after night, her slight nerves fading within minutes of being on stage. She danced with enthusiasm beneath the beams from the hot spotlight overhead that drenched her in pleasure. Ballet was what she was made for, the reason she was born. She was destined for the stage and nowhere else. When she heard from Natasha of her fiancé-turned-husband's long office hours, Zaria was glad she was in an artistic field, living out her lifelong passion.

Yes, she had undeniably inherited the artistic genes from her mother. That was what made her feel the adrenaline surge after shows, sometimes unable to even sleep for hours as she dreamt of going even higher. The ugly toes had meaning behind them. When she was younger, she would get the urge to party after a show, but now she would much rather go home and sleep as soon as she could. Waking up early, sometimes catching the sunrise became a habit she grew accustomed to. But the same spirit stayed with her underneath it all. The sparkling zest for life and the love of the rare nights out was still her trademark, her true nature. She was living and breathing a ballerina's life, the one she had worshipped for what felt like forever. Each time she took to the stage was the beginning of an adventure, an adventure she venerated.

Most of the other ballerinas were distant towards her, without the least trace of warmth. Some of them did not even say hello to her when she greeted them during rehearsals. She had expected the bubble of jealousy when she got main roles but being envied was more uncomfortable than she had anticipated. Her only real friends in the Baranski were Igor and Victor. The three of them had become close and they all hung out when they could on weekends. Igor's dirty jokes during rehearsal breaks kept everyone in stitches, especially his imitations of the choreographer whenever he turned his head. Zaria told them about Sasha's latest record attempt for which he was trying to eat the maximum number of cockroaches in one minute. The narration had them in splits, and they told her that her friend sounded like quite a character.

Zaria was next assigned the role of Princess Aurora in *Sleeping Beauty*. Dancers were given their schedules a year in advance, but she wasn't cheering when she got to know hers. She would be taking on the roles of *Cinderella,* Swanhilde in *Coppelia* and Jasmine in the new ballet *Aladdin* the next year. Despite getting commendation from Alexandr for her dancing, she currently felt a sense of deep frustration at being typecast in princessy roles. The heads of the Baranski felt that she was best suited to playing them and not the more challenging ones. She really wanted to be part of some of the abstract ballets that the group was starting to stage more often. She didn't even want to talk to anyone except Igor and Victor about this constant impatience she had to not dance the same kind of parts. But everyone told her she had to be patient, that there would be a time for everything. She grudgingly accepted it, though she still kept her hopes alive that one day she could take on different roles. Whenever she felt the frustration, she would remind herself of the hundreds of aspiring ballerinas who cried in hallways in the sheer pain of never being good enough to even get on stage.

She was nearly twenty-six and felt satisfied with her accomplishments. The money she was making gave her a lifestyle that she'd never enjoyed before. She hadn't expected to reach the heights she had this soon, but it felt well deserved. Her achievements were no small feat, drawing laurels from friends, family and critics.

At the moment Zaria felt a slight fear of ageing that was ever present even if she tried to deny it. New dancers had joined the theatre that year and younger talent was always coming. When she watched the fresh, much younger dancers at the morning rehearsals she couldn't help notice how confident they looked. Much more confident than she had been at that age.

She watched a new girl, with short blonde hair, talk almost brusquely to the rehearsal director. The girl sounded so confident and had none of the shyness that she had felt when she had just joined.

Another new American girl walked about like she owned the place and interacted with the choreographer with absolute poise. Nobody would have guessed they were new to the group had they not known it for a fact. Zaria wondered what the new recruits thought of her and the other seniors. Were they waiting for her to grow old and be cast aside?

She wasn't rehearsing that day but walked to the second rehearsal room, strongly curious to see the Baranski's latest hotshot recruit from St Petersburg—a twenty year old brunette called Anastasia. She stood near one of the chairs next to the mirrors and watched Anastasia on the floor rehearsing a solo bit for her upcoming show.

Anastasia was tall and skinny and her dark hair was gathered in a bun. Her dark eyes were framed by thick lashes and her lips were very full and rounded. Zaria watched her discuss a step with the choreographer, sounding extremely confident and not the least bit hesitant. Anastasia sprang into her routine and Zaria watched in astonishment. Her body movement was so darn good. She had perfect leaps, stunning pirouettes and seemed to move each muscle in effortless grace. Zaria stood frozen with her arms awkwardly by her side as danger bells clanged in her head. She gripped the arm of the chair, realising only minutes later that her palms were hurting from clutching too tightly.

Anastasia was already going to be taking on principal roles and was now the most high profile young star with the Baranski. She was being touted as the biggest prodigy in Russia since the unmatchable Katya herself. When she finished her routine Zaria heard someone clapping loudly.

She saw that it was Alexandr who was applauding and he continued doing so.

"*Otlichno*!" he said, beaming broadly.

Zaria felt a stab of jealousy when she heard that, since Alexandr hardly used "Excellent," to compliment even the best dancers. Anastasia was clearly much more accomplished than she, Zaria, was, at her age. She also had a much better, slimmer figure and was of course, years younger. Zaria had beaten her out for one part due to her experience and ever since, Anastasia had exhibited a wall of frostiness towards her.

Anastasia strode over to the chair next to which Zaria was standing and grabbed her white towel to wipe the sweat from her face. She started mopping her brow and Zaria in that instant knew she was standing next to her biggest competition. She felt insecure around this girl and realised instinctively that she would have a run for her money with her around.

"Hello Anastasia," Zaria said, finding that she was sounding unfriendly without intending it.

"Hi," Anastasia replied, looking up at her.

"So, um, you're now contracted?" Zaria asked, hoping the answer was no.

"Yes, I have a contract for five years," Anastasia said with a smug grin as she walked back to the floor.

Zaria felt a jolt hit her. Wow. Five years. Most others like her were on contracts that lasted three years at the most. She walked out of the room slowly, feeling that her place as Alexandr's favourite was in certain jeopardy.

In addition to this complication, Anastasia and Zaria soon found themselves locked in competition for the same parts since Alexandr thought they were suited for similar types of roles. Anastasia or Ms Nasty, as Zaria liked to think of her, had also once thrown a fit saying she wanted to do Zaria's part on an upcoming tour. Even though Alexandr hadn't paid attention to her demands, Zaria felt Anastasia's behaviour was diva-like and really unnecessary. After all, it wasn't like she was trying to sabotage Anastasia's career. which was predicted to zoom up even higher very soon. Jealousy did rise its evil, sharp claws way too often in the dance arena. She herself felt green-eyed sometimes. So what? But she never invented petty gossip about other dancers the way many did and never started false rumours. Gossip. That was all people loved to do. Rip each other apart. Now the latest rumour about Katya doing the rounds at neck-breaking speed was that she was the mistress of some married billionaire. According to some dancers she had also had plastic surgery and liposuction many years ago. Most of what was said about her was actually made up by her jealous contemporaries. Katya had wanted to be a gymnast growing up but a back injury at age nine made her switch over to ballet. Not that Zaria or anyone sympathised with her, since Katya was just too big for anyone to care.

Chapter 15

Zaria visited her mother one Sunday at her flat and immediately perceived something different about her. Her mother's face looked altered. It seemed brighter and less serious.

"You seem to be in a good mood, mama," Zaria remarked as she sat at the table and watched her mother, noticing that she was wearing eyeliner and perfume after a many years and looking relaxed.

Irina turned around from the kitchen counter and looked at her daughter with a shy expression.

"Well, it's Andrei. I really like him. He's taking me to the opera next week," Irina said with a small smile as she brought two cups of coffee in white mugs to the table.

"I'm so happy for you!" Zaria said, genuinely meaning it.

Irina sat down in the chair right next to her and they both started sipping their hot coffees. Zaria knew that Andrei was someone

Olga had introduced Irina to a few months ago. He was a middle class businessman and her mother had mentioned that they'd grown close very quickly.

She had noticed a gradual but certain change over the past few months. Her mother was now smiling much more often and looked visibly more relaxed. The anxieties that were beneath the lines on her face seemed to have diminished. She was taking more care of her appearance and in the way she dressed, something she had neglected when she had been widowed.

Both women sipped their coffees and chatted about Zaria's week. Zaria said that she was looking forward to visiting India during the Baranski's off season in winter. She now had the money for trips and wanted to be in Chennai every winter holiday.

The relentless pressure to stay thin was something Zaria felt mounting intensely as time went on. The Baranski made it mandatory for all dancers to weigh themselves every single week. No one was allowed to gain even a few pounds or it would be certain danger for their role. Despite sticking religiously to her diet, Zaria couldn't control the occasional nibble of cheese and chocolates. She then felt wracked with guilt and would try to skip a meal one weekend or try to exercise it off at the Baranski's gym.

One morning, she stepped on the scale during the Baranski's weigh in and got a huge fright. The scale showed that she had gained one whole kilogram. *Shit*. Had she gained that much since the last public weigh in a month ago? She cringed, hoping the new rehearsal director wouldn't scream at her.

"Lose that weight immediately. Or you won't fit into your costume," the stocky director who recorded all the dancers' weights said, her voice angry. She glared at Zaria, who felt like sinking into the floor.

"I'm really, really sorry ma'am. I will lose the weight. I promise. I'll um, work out more…" Zaria muttered, her voice even smaller than she felt.

Alexandr didn't pull her up for it but just told her to work the weight off. Zaria, however, was now really scared. Where was the time to work out? She had no time to hit the gym and she had to drop the kilo immediately. She didn't want to be sent packing for being overweight. That would be the most humiliating thing. For the next week, she was tentative with every bite she ate, skipping lunch one Sunday and trying to eat only as much as was necessary. Still her weight didn't go down.

That night after stuffing herself with chicken, vegetables and pasta for dinner, she walked over to the round, steel basin. Without pausing to think, she clutched the side of the basin with her right hand and forced her left ring finger and middle finger down her throat. When the nausea started, she vomited, the disgusting smell making her go on and on, unable to stop. She heard herself heaving repeatedly, in disbelief at the danger she was putting herself in, yet not trying to stop it. She let the tap water run and continued to heave until her stomach was empty.

The bulimia stuck with her, despite the heavy guilt she harboured at breaking the promise to her mother that she would never fall victim to an eating disorder. It was over three months since it had begun its hold on her. The disease attached itself to her like a leech, sucking some of her health along with it. Every time she ate a morsel, she was calculating how many calories she would gain with it. Due to the ruthless suppression of her appetite, she sometimes felt she had to binge a little and then throw up to keep her weight down. It had been three months since she first threw up her meal and it had continued, leaving her unable to push the stop button. She found herself throwing up many of her meals after eating a lot, especially dinners after shows. She felt drained at times, but had lost the weight she had gained and kept her place in the group. Her body now looked skinnier, almost touching on the border of emaciated. When her mother asked about it, she lied saying that she was just on a tight diet for a short while longer. She felt dehydrated from the vomiting and her teeth became eroded on the surface. But still, the satisfaction of staying thin made her continue the vomiting. The dark abyss dragged her in deeper and deeper, and because of her desperation to stay in the group, she let it pull her down. One part of her was screaming to stop her madness, but she didn't listen to those cries.

The stress and feeling of being deprived of food built up, but she didn't give them a second thought. She had lost the weight and was determined to stay skinny, no matter what. Occasional bouts of depression came, but she never once thought of confiding in a friend. Not once did she reach out to anyone. She had to become thinner.

A turning point occurred when her periods became irregular. She missed one menstrual cycle and started worrying about her body. At first, she thought she was pregnant and panicked but the pregnancy test turned up negative. Her periods had been irregular for awhile but right then she knew her body was nowhere near to being okay. That was when she woke up and began to see what was happening to her. She didn't realise how the disease was taking over her life, changing her into a demon and sucking her life away. But she was out of control. The alarm bells clanged louder and louder in her head, as her conscience screamed out for her to listen. She heard them, and then wanted some help in controlling herself, but she couldn't.

One night, her mother caught her throwing up soon after dinner. Irina had walked in to see her daughter standing over the basin and then washing her mouth of stains.

"Sweetheart, are you okay? Why are you vomiting?" Irina asked, coming up to her and placing a hand on her shoulder.

Zaria turned to face her, aware that the sickness in her expression would give away her crime. Her eyes looked blank and helpless, devoid of energy. She glanced at her left hand, which had scars on the knuckles from sticking the fingers down her throat to induce vomiting. The small mirror above the basin showed the pimples and rashes on her face. She tried to choke back tears, knowing that she desperately needed help. She braced herself before speaking.

"I did it on purpose. I can't help it," she confessed, her voice pained. Her throat ached and she swallowed, feeling nervous. Then the tears broke free and started trickling down her cheeks.

Irina froze and just stared at her for a few moments, looking stunned as the significance of the words sank in.

Then she flew at her daughter, slapping her on her cheek. She slapped her again and again so hard until Zaria's face hurt and stung all over.

"How dare you! You promised never to…" Irina screamed as she hit her again. Zaria just stood there, her tears flowing faster, not attempting to dodge her mother's blows.

Irina stopped her hand in midair and let it fall down limply to her side. The rage in her eyes disappeared and turned into extreme worry. Her expression became crestfallen. She started crying, sobbing noisily. Then she stepped forward and hugged her daughter to her chest.

Zaria broke down.

"It's been on for a few months. Help me mama. I don't know how else to stay thin," she whimpered between sobs, clutching her mother tight.

"Ssshhhh," was all Irina said as she held her and stroked her hair. She sat Zaria down on the couch and spoke to her for nearly an hour. She showed no anger, but instead tenderly explained the facts to Zaria like she was a child once more. She was, however, firm that Zaria get professional help to overcome her disorder.

The next morning, Irina took her to a doctor specialising in eating disorders, sitting with her while the doctor explained how dangerous a position she had put herself in. Zaria took the doctor's advice on getting back to normalcy seriously. She had to ensure she followed the list of foods she had to eat to repair her body—probiotics found in yoghurt, buttermilk, Omega-3 fatty acids, oats, brown rice and more things she couldn't remember. Her mother was the one who stuck the list up on her fridge and made sure she forced all those things into her body. Very gradually, Zaria started inching back to eating normally. Her mother made her honestly recite what she had eaten everyday at the Baranski's canteen on the phone. She also took Zaria to a dietician who gave her a list of healthy diets she could follow if she wanted to lose weight. She forced her to see a therapist a few times a month, which they kept quiet from the people at the Baranski. Zaria's teeth slowly improved after a few consultations with a dental care specialist. She resolved to nurse her body back to shape, so that it could regain the strength it had been drained of. She also made time to work out when she could and decided to just go on a stern diet the next time she had a weight problem. To think of how far she had let herself fall made her shudder.

Irina drilled it into her repeatedly to promise never to become bulimic again. Such an ugly word, Zaria realised only now.

"I promise," she said.

Chapter 16

A group of ballet dancers from the Baranski were going to tour India that winter, having received an invite from the Indian Cultural Department. Zaria was delighted to be a part of it. She went to Chennai a week before the rest of the group, since it was her vacation time and she intended to spend it there as usual.

This time, she was staying with her grandmother, whom she had grown closer to over the past few years. Since her husband's death, Jaya had lost much of her stern nature.

"How much *dhristi* there is on you now that you are so successful," Jaya started as she sat in her old rocking chair clad in a peach sari.

Zaria laughed and shook her head as she sat on the smooth surface of the table next to her. Her grandmother's eyes were less harsh and her face was more lined but the small, round red kumkum sat on her forehead as always.

"Irina, I must say…She actually has a trace of Rajiv's nature in her," Jaya suddenly said, looking at Irina.

The mention of his name resulted in a thick silence. For a few moments no one spoke. Then Irina got up and sat down in the chair next to Jaya.

"You won't believe this Jaya…That is just what I wanted to tell you," she said very softly, taking Jaya's hand in hers.

The old woman smiled at her and did not say anything for some time. The man they both missed was the one common link between them, something they had never brought up ever before. They both shared a knowing smile for a moment. One that Zaria was glad to see. The three of them continued chatting about their other family members and recent weddings that had taken place in the city.

Irina had told her daughter the whole truth of why she had had to leave India after her husband's death only a few months ago. Zaria had, at first, felt completely shocked at hearing the way her mother had been treated and had felt upset at her grandparents for their callous behaviour. She'd nearly cried as she thought of the cruelty her mother had been forced to deal with all alone. But Irina had calmed her down and told her to forget the past completely.

"Don't hold the past against anyone. No point in raking up unpleasant memories," she had said.

Zaria quietly understood and respected her mother's wishes. Her grandparents had always loved her, she knew, despite their non-acceptance of her mother. As she watched her mother and grandmother sitting side by side, mental pictures of her mother's difficulties following her father's death flashed before her eyes.

After Rajiv's fatal accident and demise, Irina looked like she had aged overnight. A cloud of gloom and fear hung over her. Grief filled her being and suffocated her. Losing the person she had loved more than her life was unbearable. She could barely register the fact that Rajiv was gone. The void left by his death was so large, so bloody. It was a horror that had transformed her life, ripping the love and safety she had been wrapped in. She was thrown into a volcano of sorrow and loneliness from a mountaintop of luxury.

The phone rang incessantly less than a day later. House mortgaged. Heavy loans. Irina tried to stay standing as the meaning hit her. Rajiv had not told her all that he had sacrificed to give them their lifestyle. She called her banker for some hope but was lashed by yet another blow. She was unaware of the bad investments that Rajiv had made. He had kept the news of his bad fortunes hidden from her, not wanting to burden her with worry. He had lost nearly half of his savings over the past year. She had nothing to fall back on.

Rajiv had not told her, knowing that when he took over the business in less than a year, these things could be taken care of. Whatever was left in the bank in Rajiv's name had to be used to pay off the bank debts. Irina was left with nothing, not even a penny to her name.

She broke down in the privacy of her room as she regretted how freely she had spent, how lavish she had been. How foolish they had both been. Now she could not give her daughter the same standard of living the child was used to since birth. How could they even live? Rajiv had no personal assets and whatever was there had been repossessed by the bank. In short she was bankrupt. Penniless.

Her mother-in-law then summoned her to her house and sat her down in the drawing room. Irina took one look at her chilly expression and trembled. She now felt more scared of the woman than ever.

"I don't have to spell out the mess you are in. I am willing to provide for Zaria. She is, after all, our grandchild. But I will lay down some conditions and expect you to follow them implicitly," Jaya said, her eyes stern as she looked at Irina.

"If you agree to bring the child up in Madras, the way we want her to be brought up, you can stay on in our house with her, as her mother. But mind you, if you decide to bring her up independently, here or in Russia, we refuse to support you," she said. She immediately followed it up with a long list of 'dos' and 'don'ts' for Irina, which she would have to comply with if she wanted her in-laws' support.

Her husband who sat next to her nodded quietly, echoing her sentiments as always, not even uttering one word of sympathy for Irina or her plight.

Irina gripped her hands together, tight, so much that they hurt. She tried not to faint. How was she to raise her child now? Her in-laws thought that she did not have the right to anything. Living under their roof, she would feel like a prisoner. She would not have a say in her daughter's life or upbringing and would always be an unwanted third.

"We do want the best for our grandchild so if you both stay here we will ensure that she has the best of everything. Not if you take her away," Jaya reiterated, accenting each word, loudly and forcefully. Irina opened her mouth to protest but not even a sound, a whisper came forth.

She shrunk back from the sofa across, wanting to go as far away from the woman as she could. She was now too scared to even be angry. Why did they have to be so cruel to her just because she was not their choice? She knew she would have to struggle and work to bring her child up, but how? She was qualified for almost nothing. She took another glance at Jaya's cold gaze and knew she could never live with such animosity around her. She had never felt so lonely. She needed the security and love of her parents and knew they would give her the support that she craved for. Though she wanted to stay in India she could see no way of doing so.

She called her parents in Moscow. They were, as expected, extremely supportive and promised that they would help her raise her child. That forced her to make a life-changing decision for Zaria, though it meant uprooting the child from familiar surroundings and forcing her into a new culture completely alien to her.

Zaria shook herself free from the morbid pictures of the past that came uninvited. She observed that her grandmother and mother were talking with genuine warmth, without any coldness or bitterness visible in their visage. This made her marvel at her mother's gentle, forgiving nature. She had noticed how Jaya's hard stance towards Irina had slowly thawed over the years and had been replaced by grudging admiration. Now, she was truly warmer and loving towards her and in fact, they sometimes spoke on the phone about Zaria. The past could never be altered, could not be erased, but at least something could be salvaged in the present.

Zaria picked on her bowl of sweet melons with a fork and noticed her mother watching her out of the corner of her eye. She was grateful that her mother had kept her promise not to mention her bulimia scare to anyone.

After finishing her melons she left the room to let Jaya watch her favourite Tamil serial on Sun TV. Irina stayed and both women talked and talked some more.

Chennai's landscape had changed a bit since the last time Zaria had visited. The plethora of posters and billboards everywhere remained but the city now had a few new malls and cineplexes. Zaria loved the way all these things were coming up and making the city more fun to visit. Each time she returned to Chennai, she felt closer to it. Whenever she sat in the car she loved to take in everything as she drove by on the roads crowded with heavy traffic. Zaria loved everything about the city, especially the culture that existed hand-in-hand with westernisation. Most of her friends partied at nightclubs almost non-stop every night and she joined them, wanting to make the most of her off season. She did a short ballet workshop with children at the Russian Cultural Centre. The little ones were very excited to meet a ballerina who lived so far away.

The monsoon season was just drawing to a close, the heavy rains slowing down and tapering off. The weather was cool and just gorgeous. How she loved being in Chennai at this time of the year. After her daily stretches, Zaria took early morning walks in the garden when the frost and dew hung in the air. She wore loose T-shirts and roomy pants whenever she walked. She wore loose clothing more often now, wanting to let her muscles breathe with their constant exertion. On some days a light drizzle fell which gave her the chance to curl up indoors with a DVD. She also spent hours reading Tolstoy's famous novel, *War and Peace* which her grandfather had given her some years ago. The book enchanted her with its story of romance, counts, princes and Russian historical culture that she loved. Surprising, she had hated reading it when she was a younger, more impatient youth.

Her story had generated a huge buzz in the city, as her accomplishments were being discussed by family members over coffees and dinners. The fact that a girl from the city was now a ballerina with the famous Baranski Ballet had piqued the interest of the local media. A city newspaper interviewed her and the article that was subsequently published described her as a unique achiever. It gushed about her beauty and the fact that she had made it from early childhood struggles and a move far away. Zaria was extremely flattered and touched by India's love and warmth towards her. It was as though they wanted to adopt her. At times like these, Zaria felt a deeper connection with India than what she had known growing up.

She did a photo shoot and an interview for a city lifestyle magazine. She posed in a number of silk saris and when the edition was out with her on the cover, she even received an offer to work in a Tamil movie. In a country where fair skin was an obsession, her very pale skin and green eyes were what filmmakers apparently found fascinating. She turned down the offers though it was heart-warming to feel so well accepted. Since she was now quite well off with her earnings from ballet, no one in the family asked her things like, "Why don't you get a job?" This was a question some Indians asked her when she was yet to make it.

In India, Zaria cherished her childhood friendships and family ties very highly, which created a sheltering wall around her. She never felt this protected and cared for in Moscow or anywhere else in the world. At the same time, she thought about how fortunate her mother and she were at the present stage in their lives. They had both now found a sense of peace, a sense of belonging in their journeys. Irina had since started reviewing the odd ballet for a newspaper and said she enjoyed writing very much. She had also started living with Andrei for the past five months, and their relationship was fast becoming more serious. Zaria felt so happy that her mother had found love again, though she said that no one could ever replace Rajiv in her heart.

As Zaria did her daily stretches, she did exercises to specifically strengthen her feet, since her left one was still weak. She didn't want to risk another injury to her left foot, knowing it could spell the end of her stage life. Doctors had warned her that another serious injury to that foot could jeopardise her career. She did an exercise that Alexandr had advised her to do. She sat barefoot in her room and tried to grab the carpet on the floor with her feet. Then she stretched her toes from one side to the other, trying to form a fist. Alexandr had also told her about many other exercises to help her foot, ankle and toes get more strength. The rest of her body felt good, but she was always somewhat concerned about her left foot being fragile.

The rest of the group members from the Baranski arrived in Chennai soon and Zaria was happy to be their tour guide. She showed them some of the famous temples in the city with their elaborately carved sculptures. Everyone remarked that Indians came across as very hospitable and welcoming. Igor and Victor came over to Zaria's aunt's house and met her family. Zaria mentioned that the two guys were so close to her that they were like her own brothers. She updated both of them about Sasha's latest wacky attempt. This had everybody in hysterics.

The Baranski was to perform in Chennai and then in Bombay, Delhi and Bangalore. Zaria had only committed to the two shows in Chennai, and another dancer was doing her part in the remaining shows on the tour. She didn't want to spend her holidays touring and Alexandr had agreed to her request.

The tickets for the ballet *La Bayadere* sold out and it went off smoothly, though they had only rehearsed once with the orchestra. The story had an Indian touch which was why Zaria felt it was really special to dance it in India, in front of her family and friends. They received a standing ovation that lasted long and she couldn't have felt in higher spirits than she did that evening. She was home.

Two days later, Ashwin asked her out once again, to her surprise. She said yes, though she was only in town for a few more weeks. Tara and Gul teased her about it but for all the fuss they were making, what happened wasn't very serious. Zaria just went out with Ashwin on a few dates around the city. She found him strikingly handsome with his tanned brown complexion that she always found attractive in guys. And he was a really good kisser. It helped that they were both already close friends, and could talk easily about anything. She remembered when he tried to do very romantic things like send her five bouquets of red roses on her birthday in Moscow some years ago. His persistence is pursuing her was more flattering than anything else.

Ashwin took her out to dinner a few times, and each time Zaria was hoping no one her mother knew would spot them. She didn't want people in Chennai to start gossiping about the two of them having an affair.

One day, Ashwin was watching a One Day International cricket match at his house, while Zaria was sitting with him on the couch. They were making out and cuddling during commercial breaks, and she loved running her hands through his thick curls. Ashwin, however, grew increasingly obsessed with the commentary and action on the screen and started ignoring her. He kept munching on chocolate chip cookies, his eyes glued to the screen. Zaria playfully tried to distract Ashwin by standing in front of the TV, and even dancing seductively in front of it, but he shoved her out of the way. She finally threw a pillow at him and gave up.

"This is so ridiculous…it can't be normal," she said, shaking her head, though she smiled too.

"It totally is. I am determined to be the most obsessed cricket fan there is," Ashwin said, putting his arm around her.

He didn't even want to go out to the beach when the match was finishing saying, "I have to know how it ends."

Irina approved of Ashwin because he wasn't into drugs or excessive smoking and alcohol. She considered those kind of *good* kids rare. She liked him even more because he was very polite.

When it was time for Zaria to go back to Moscow, Ashwin saw her off at the airport. That was the end of their short time together. Another rich man after her, well that was her luck. But he was so far away and she could never see him. Being unlucky in love seemed to be what she had to get used to, sad as that sounded.

Chapter 17

Months later, Irina and Andrei took their marriage vows in a synagogue. The ceremony was a very quiet one with Galya and Zaria being the only witnesses present. Both of them watched as the marriage contract called the *ketuba* was signed. Andrei gave Irina a ring under the wedding canopy and then the groom broke a glass with his right foot. As Zaria watched the bride and groom with the Rabbi, she knew her mother had finally found that sense of fulfilment which she had given up trying to find. Seeing her marrying another man did not give Zaria any twinges of discomfort. She instead felt a huge surge of happiness for her mother who had found true love once more. Life had changed for both women. They were both in new, more contented phases of their lives. Zaria had risen steadily and felt she was now in a great phase in her career. Fate had smiled on them after long years of pain. Irina, in her white wedding gown, gazed adoringly at Andrei looking radiant and very much in love. Her cheeks had tears flowing down them, glistening brightly. After her marriage, she would live just an hour away from her daughter.

It had been over a year since Zaria had understood the danger she had to haul herself away from. Her eating disorder was now more under control, as her mother supervised everything she ate and ensured she didn't throw up. Zaria forced herself to eat a little when she felt like skipping a meal. To think that she could have ended up stuck in the deep hole of that disease made her tremble. It was one secret she was too ashamed to discuss with anyone.

One afternoon during a rehearsal break, Alexandr suddenly clapped his hands. All heads from various corners of the room turned towards him. Most of the dancers were sitting down on the wooden benches or drinking water. Zaria stopped midway through wiping sweat off her neck.

Alexandr's expression suddenly looked so heavy, so serious. What was he going to say?

"Everyone, my dear friends…my family…I am going to be leaving you soon…" Alexandr began.

He was cut short by loud gasps. Zaria was too shell-shocked to even hear his words. "Going to head a group in Germany. Heartbroken to leave…Will always remember my extraordinary time here."

She watched as Alexandr was mobbed by everyone in the room who gave him goodbye hugs. She heard everyone echoing her thoughts. We will really miss you. Our favourite director to work with.

"Thank you," was all Zaria could say as she hugged him before he was smothered by more people.

"I will be in touch with you all on e-mail. You can ask me for advice anytime," Alexandr said with his signature smile.

He had been the head and chief brains of the Baranski for nearly six years. Zaria tried to hold her tears back. She remembered the impromptu dinners he would have at his home to make dancers feel like they were a part of his family. He had become a mentor to so many young dancers…more especially to her.

She realised after a few hours that his departure made everything so much more problematic for her. He was the one who had brought her where she was, carved her rise. And the worst part was that Alexandr had just said that she could try and take on a role in a contemporary ballet, i.e. ballet which has elements of modern dance also, a genre that the group was going to put up for the first time the next season. She had been so happy to hear it. But now he was leaving. She felt like breaking something, but then tried to accept that those kind of ballets may never happen to her. She was so frustrated that she was in a foul mood for two whole days. So close. So close.

"India is just so wonderful. I'll tell you about it later," Zaria said to a new girl as she massaged her body herself by lying on a rubber ball and rolling. She closed her eyes and took in the pleasing sensation of her back muscles being rolled by the ball. She had to teach the way she danced a role to the new girl, who would be dancing the part that season.

"India sounds so interesting…" the girl stated with wide eyes as she rolled her muscles out on a foam roller. The air of youthful wonder at the beginning of her career was all about her, reminding Zaria of a younger version of herself.

"Zaria! Anna! That's enough! Get to the bars now!" a loud, imposing voice snapped as the Baranski's new director walked in, making Zaria rush to the bar immediately.

Boris' was nearly five years older than Alexandr and had long, greying blonde hair and thick eyebrows. His eyes were steely like his military manner. He had a thickset face and a square jaw. He was a highly venerated name in ballet, a former legend from St Petersburg who had created several ballets at the Balshoy. His voice had a commanding, almost scary ring to it when he shouted. He took dancers apart in front of everyone if they didn't meet his standards, making the unease prompt them to work harder. He rarely complimented dancers and getting one flattering remark from him was considered a huge accomplishment.

The newfound hindrance made Zaria more determined to stay where she was. Alexandr had made her too comfortable with her abilities, and an unforgiving director was just what she needed. At rehearsals she continued to work hard, and hoped that she wouldn't be a victim of Boris' next public battering.

Her bulimia was now completely behind her, thanks to her mother's intervention. She was finally back to normal and felt much wiser for her rash mistake. It was over. She knew she would never do it again. Ever. She had been shaken up by the experience, but knew it had changed her for the better. She realised that she had to let go of her ego and think about the huge mistake she had committed. It had resulted in a side of her that had made her think about herself, think of how she should perhaps become a little rational.

That season, she was the recipient of the "Soul of Dance award" in the "Rising star" category from the Russian Ballet Council. It was a very major award, given to a Russian ballerina once a year. Along with the acclaim she had got for her recent shows, this plaque added to the high she was on. She felt she was riding a purple patch that seemed to stretch on into the distance.

Despite her climax, Zaria had another thorn in her mind. She had tried many times to flirt with Boris, but he didn't seem to be aware of her charms at all. He was instead very engrossed in Anastasia and rumours were already swirling that they were both an item. Zaria was extremely disappointed to hear this but felt helpless, watching. She knew that at this point, dating someone like him would have given her career a boost like no other.

She sat in her silky fur coat in the back seat of the limousine that had been sent for her. The plush leather seats were spacious and she leaned back, enjoying the opulence in the chauffeur driven vehicle. As the limousine rambled along the smooth, wide roads to the Kremlin Theatre, she glanced out of the window. The sky was steadily turning darker, the blackness emerging and the stars starting to peer out. The cool air blowing lightly on her face made her anticipate the significant night ahead. She spotted a gypsy on the roadside, in her dusty, flowery blouse and long skirt. Her earrings were large hoops, and brought to mind mystery and curiosity.

She found her gaze drift away from the windows and turn inwards, towards some uncertainties she felt. If she wanted to stay a principal dancer she had to keep dancing to her form. The Baranski had more than a few new dancers with young blood injected into it that year. Anastasia looked set to become ballet's biggest star and she was already a national sensation. She was becoming a serious threat, despite Zaria trying to tell herself it wasn't true.

Zaria recalled a phone conversation she had had with Olga just a couple of weeks ago. She had confided her uncertainties about ageing to her mentor.

"My dear child, don't be so worried about approaching twenty-six. Every dancer must go through it and you can be amongst those who stay right where they are. Look at the plus points. Your technique is still strong, your body is holding up and your beauty and figure remain Though you are not amongst the younger dancers anymore, there are active dancers who are over thirty…" Olga had said in an understanding manner.

Zaria had nodded and thanked her before hanging up. She had felt a lot better after Olga's wise advice and tried to listen to it. The oldest dancer in the group was in fact thirty-five. No problem. Okay.

They drove past the Kremlin, with cathedrals of striking Russian architecture. The Cathedral of the Dormition had five golden coloured domes and resembled an old cultural relic. The Cathedral of the Annunciation was a nine domed edifice, with a tall white-stone porch on the southern side. On the northern and western sides, the Cathedral had beautifully carved portals done by Russian masters in the 16thcentury. The Great Kremlin Palace had a façade of dull golden brown on the walls with white underneath the curves of the windows. The window surrounds had carving on white stone while the plinth wall was made of rustic stone.

When they drove past the Kremlin Palace of Congress Zaria gazed at the building, appreciating its beauty. On the outside, the vertical wooden panels glowed lightly in the night. The effect against the night sky was of a soft brown and gold blending harmoniously into the skyline. A coat of arms of the Soviet Union hung over the main entrance on the façade. In the upper part, the spaces between the windows carried the emblems of emancipated labour, peace and socialism, made of golden mosaic enamel.

Someone held the door open for her and said, "Welcome, ma'am" in a respectful tone.

She stepped out in her coat, boots and woollen gloves. She remembered coming by the palace as a child and watching the changing of the guards who marched, lifting their legs far too high for her liking. She had giggled, until her mother had smiled and murmured to her not to point.

She felt like she was at the pre-eminent time in her career at present. She had won a recent big ballet competition and was getting glowing reviews for her current show. Things couldn't get any better. Even in her personal life things were looking really rosy. She was now dating a man called Leonid, a wealthy businessman who owned many upscale stores in the city. They had met at a Baranski fundraiser only five months ago but were already very close. She had a feeling that this relationship had something more to it than the others, right from their very first date.

That evening, she sat back on the large couch in the dressing room, listening to soft music on her iPod. Months had passed since the Kremlin show had taken place, but she could still feel the afterglow of it, and couldn't forget how mindblowing it had been to perform there. She hummed softly in tune to the music, basking in the high she was on. She was backstage as usual after having had her makeup done, getting geared up for another show. The show would be starting in about twenty minutes according to her watch. She heard a knock on her door and turned her head towards it.

"Yes I'm ready!" she called out, loudly and clearly.

"Good. Fifteen minutes," the stage manager said through the thick brown door.

Zaria took off her iPod headphones from her ears and placed them on the dressing table. She spotted her special ventilated shoe bag near the couch, walked over and sat down. Opening the bag, she pulled out one shoe and turned it over in the air, to check if the sole was all right. A sudden noise of glass hitting the floor made her glance down.

She nearly screamed. Small pieces of glass were falling out from the inside of her shoes. She recoiled as she stared at the razor sharp shards, their uneven edges casting shadows onto the carpet. Her pupils widened as a gasp escaped her. She let her shoe fall to the floor, hearing it crunch over the glass. Light from her dressing table glistened off the edges of some glass shards. They were pointed. Sharp. She stumbled back with a gasp, stepping away. *Fuck*. Sharp glass. *Glass*. In her shoe. To cut her. To make her bleed.

Her mind blurred. Thoughts flew fast and thick through it. She felt faint and had to steady herself by holding onto the arm of a chair. What was she to think? Someone had put crushed glass in her shoes, in order to cut her feet. To seriously injure her. Some jealous rival had obviously done it, wanting to put her out of commission. But who? Who? Her habit of inspecting the sole every time had saved her from gashes on her feet. Otherwise her feet would be bloodied and torn now, with glass sticking out of her toes. The image made her shudder. Her eyes started welling up. She suddenly felt so alone, terrified, unable to believe what was happening. She had heard of an American ballerina falling victim to this crushed glass attack and not being able to dance for so many months. Disgusting what some people would do. But they had wanted to hurt her badly. To bring her crashing down.

The air grew cold suddenly, almost icy. A tremor ran through her, making her whole body convulse. A thick teardrop escaped her eye and trickled slowly down her long lashes. No, she had to control herself. She couldn't cry. She tried to blink away the tears. However disturbed her aura of confidence was, she had to keep her head. Whichever bitch had tried to burn her wouldn't succeed in scaring her. She would go on. Despite the severe shock. The thought of her bleeding feet once more made her petrified. Her hands shook. Yet she had to go on stage in ten minutes. She would dance, of course. No way would she crumble and give in to the witch who had done this. It had to be a she, right? But whom? How? When? Her heart was racing and she tried to take some deep breaths. She heard her shaky breath, seemingly deafening, and tried to think. Someone must have bribed someone who had access to her dressing room. But who had bribed whom? Only the dressers, makeup artist, cleaners had access…but which dancer was behind it? Anastasia perhaps? She openly hated Zaria. Anastasia had lost out on a role to her in the past. But then, it could have been any of the others. One of the girls in the show? Who? Who?

She shook her head. No time to think of who was behind it. They had just succeeded in provoking her. How dare someone try to mess with her! She wouldn't give in to it, they wouldn't get her part. No way. Never.

She gingerly walked around the glass pieces to the dressing table and pulled a tissue out of the tissue box. She looked into the mirror and dabbed her eyes quickly, before proceeding to touch-up her makeup. That wasn't a problem. She knew how to do that.

Maybe she would never find out who the villain was. Maybe she could never prove who was behind it all. But right now, she had a show. She had to go on soon. She had to be strong. No need to call for help. She just had to perform. Yes, she would go on. And dance. That was what she loved. She couldn't slip up or tell anyone that she had cried. She didn't want to.

Chapter 18

Zaria grabbed her other pair of shoes from the shoe cupboard near the dressing table. She hurriedly wrenched them out of the box and bent one quickly from the heel. She then started hitting the toe box of the shoe on the wooden door of her dressing room. She hadn't broken in a new shoe this way since she was eleven. She hit with all her might, venom and frustration as she swung the shoe again and again. How silly of her, to take her anger out on the shoe. She heard the soft thud, like someone was dusting, as she pounded the shoe on the door. She then hurriedly slipped the shoes on. An almost new pair still felt so hard, how would she manage dancing in these? She had worn them only twice before this during practices. Once was for a rehearsal a day earlier, but they still didn't feel fully broken in. What if she hurt herself? But there wasn't time to think or fret. She had to dance.

She stepped hastily to the barres backstage and put her right foot up, trying hard to stay composed while she stretched. Her costume fit well, she had only worn it once before. Her legs felt a little stiff as she stretched them, as did the shoes on her feet. The dresser walked past her and Zaria muttered to her about the glass pieces in her shoes in the dressing room, drawing a quizzical look.

Zaria looked around at the other dancers getting ready backstage. No one spoke to her before a show, as they knew she liked to be alone with her thoughts then. She looked from one to the other, watching everyone brushing strands off their face and pulling themselves together. She barely heard the bulky costume mistress, who was giving an intense lecture to a dancer who had gotten a small tear in her tutu. Who could have been the one behind the sabotage attempt? Was it the new girl with short hair whose name she didn't know? She didn't look ruffled as she stretched, but maybe she was not a likely villain. Could it have been Anya or Svetlana? They both kept calm expressions as they whispered to each other. Perhaps it was one of the girls in the corps de ballet, someone who wanted to get bigger. Anastasia was the one she suspected strongly but she wasn't there, she wasn't in the show. Zaria would have loved to have seen her expression right then, to see if she betrayed herself.

She somehow forced herself to shove these thoughts aside and prayed mentally that she could compose herself and pull this one off.

The show began. She was playing Giselle in the Gothic story of the peasant girl whose ghost had to protect her love, after her death, from spirits. Giselle fell in love with a peasant, who she didn't know was Count Albrecht in disguise. Zaria's mind was still on the severe shock she had received minutes earlier. She felt off-colour and knew she must look peculiar as she danced. She tried to focus but didn't smile as much as she should have when she danced her love duet. Forget the glass, you're playing Giselle, she told herself, trying to get her mind off the backstage scare.

Just then she heard a rip near her thighs as she leapt in the air. *Fuck. Her costume torn already, in the first act itself.* The tear was towards the back, it wasn't visible to the audience at least. But she felt a draft there and was irritated with herself for ripping her costume so early. She tried to smile and continue but knew she wasn't performing as well as she normally did. She must have looked out of place, like she didn't belong there. In the small room near the wings, she managed the costume change okay for her next scene. When Giselle discovered her love's secret, that he was actually a Count who was betrothed, she lost her mind and died of a broken heart. The dim spotlight shone down on Zaria as she was the lone figure in the centre of the stage. The crowd was not visible in the darkness, their faces all covered in shadows. She forced the thoughts of the glass out of her head, and being a professional, didn't get distracted too much.

In the Second Act, she had to enter as the ghost of Giselle who rose from her grave at night. She fidgeted with her shoes backstage. The left one was too tight, her toes felt cramped and achy. By the time she took the left shoe off and put it on again, she had missed her entry. She forgot to enter! Great! How idiotic was that, the main character entering late while the rest of the cast improvised and went on with the show.

She made her late entry and danced her part as Giselle who watched over her beloved, protecting him from the Wilis—female spirits who were jilted before their weddings. The spirits rose at night from their graves to get their revenge on men by dancing them to death. Zaria was still seething. How could she mess up such an important part? She finally was going to get the chance to do some different roles, break out of the fairy mould she had been wedged in for years. Vanya said she was making note of her hard work and would help her do something different very soon. Boris agreed and told her that he would let her try out for a role she wanted after a few months. But she had to prove she could do them and if this was the way she danced…Ughh.

The second act went much better than the first. She forced herself to forget her previous blunders and dance with all her polish, her usual spunk. The story was gothic—of brides who died before their weddings rising from their graves. She was playing a ghost now. With the scare she had just received she must have looked the part without trying.

Later, as she was doing a series of pirouettes, her left foot slipped and she fell down awkwardly. Her knee took the impact of the sudden fall and she felt the excruciating pain hit her. She kept her expression as calm as possible and smiled widely as the dancers behind her swept her back onto her feet in a smooth motion. She went on, thrusting the moment of disturbed momentum out of her mind. But she felt that weakness surface, that ringing feeling of vulnerability. How clumsy she must have looked, she thought. Titters must have burst out from all who were watching when she tripped. Thankfully, she danced all right for the remaining part of the show, finishing it without adding to her misery.

The applause was polite for her and louder for the male lead. She kept her head high and her smile stuck on her face as she bowed. Inside, she was miffed. How disgusting she must have looked falling down like that. She had that feeling a dancer got when she knew a show had not gone well. On the other hand, she didn't remember making too many mistakes. So perhaps she had done okay, not as badly as she thought.

She walked to the dressing room quickly and saw that the glass had been swept up. But she paused with her left hand on the doorknob of the open door, not wanting to go inside yet.

Loud footsteps came up from behind her.

"What was that from you today? *Uzhasno*!" an angry voice commented, labelling her performance as *horrible*.

It was Boris. *Oh, shit*. Had she been that bad?

She cringed and slowly turned around, hoping he wasn't going to yell at her in front of everyone.

"I'm really, really sorry I was off today. Just a bad day. I was feeling a little sick too. It won't happen again," she said her expression pleading, her voice cracking, trying to keep tears from gushing out.

"If you were that sick you shouldn't have danced! Do you know the number of mistakes you made? There was barely any life in your dancing. Good thing this wasn't the premiere," Boris finished, giving her a look of exasperation and turning away.

Zaria tried to walk but felt a dizziness start in her head and could barely keep standing. She sat herself down on one of the chairs in the wings and stared ahead of her. Her cheeks were burning. Some other dancers were watching her from a short distance away. She didn't want to look at them and turned her face away. Maybe Anastasia would get her part soon. But no, she had done this show before so many times and done it so competently. She had to keep her place. But she couldn't hold in her tears any longer. They rolled out of her eyes and stained her cheeks. She could hear the hushed whispers from the dancers. She could feel their pitying stares. Why did it matter what they thought? As though they had never had a bad day. Did they have to stand there and stare?

She covered her face with her palms and let the tears run, the hot tears ruining her eye makeup. A hand touched her shoulder but she automatically shrugged it off, not caring who it was. Her palms felt sticky and wet, stuck close to her face as she cried. The smell of fresh paint from the prop next to her hit her nose hard, made it feel like it was going to burn. She didn't want to be a spectacle so she got up and walked into her dressing room before covering her face again as she sat on the couch. Why did she have to act like a weakling when people were watching? No one could know how she felt. She had to look strong, be strong. On the outside, she had to shrug away the problem, that's what professionals did. Everyone had a bad day, didn't they? But why did that have to be today? Her head ached terribly, making her eyes hurt too. She knew she had to stop crying but was unable to control her tears. The dresser came in and asked her to remove the tutu, saying she would stain it. Zaria wiped her face with a tissue and stood up. She helped the dresser as she peeled her costume off carefully. The lady was probably hoping she wouldn't tear this one too, she thought.

When the dresser left, she changed into her jeans and sweater but sat back down on the couch, not wanting to go out immediately.

She had to just calm down, not panic and get more hysterical. She felt compelled to tell Boris about the whole thing. Yes, then the group would have to try and find out who had tried to hurt her. But no, no that would start being gossiped about and she didn't want all the drama. Perhaps she needed to also talk to the psychiatrist the company had. Maybe the therapist could help her get over this whole episode with some counselling. She could bare her soul about the sabotage attempt and it would clear her mind up. That would get her some sympathy.

No. She couldn't appear pathetic and puny. No psychiatrist. She would talk to Leonid, tell him all about her nightmare on this bad day. He was so sweet and understanding. He would hold her and console her and make her forget all this. She felt her shock and fright melt away into a larger pot of fury. How dare someone try to mess with her? She wanted to wring that woman's neck, whoever she was. But first she had to recover from this, from the punch that had nearly knocked her out. She needn't feel so mortified about a few mistakes. She would dance so amazingly after this that the bitch who dared to try and pull her down would be confounded. And she would get back up so fast that her enemy would be the one worrying.

Next morning at rehearsal, Zaria mentioned the crushed glass episode to Boris, not showing any of the emotions she had felt on her face. Boris reacted with shock. He sounded very worried and asked if she was hurt.

"This is terrible. Someone trying to harm one of our group members. We will surely launch an investigation into this right away," he said, his voice becoming angrier with each word.

Zaria nonchalantly continued sewing ribbons on her pointe shoes and brushed the topic away.

"It was no big deal, didn't bother me," she replied with a smirk.

She didn't want to sound upset, didn't want to give her enemy that satisfaction.

"That's the right attitude," Boris said, commending her with a pat on the shoulder. He sounded pleased.

Zaria felt the triumph at doing something right, at crawling back out of her deep hole. Other than Igor and Victor, whom she had sworn to secrecy, she hadn't told anyone about the scare she had gotten. She knew if the media got wind of the news, they would blow it up. Such attention was the last thing she wanted. Boris had agreed to keep the police investigation quiet, as per her request. But her life didn't feel the same anymore. It was now plagued with questions and lurking with shadows. Her cocoon had been shattered, when she had been completely unprepared. She hadn't slept a minute the previous night, instead dwelling on how careful and guarded she would have to become. Someone in the group wanted to wring her neck. She would have to watch her back. Really watch it. Who could she even trust now? She would have to be wary of anyone who had access to her dressing room. Anyone. And was the saboteur going to try something else on her again? She wondered what that could be, knowing the incessant worrying could ruin her concentration and her career. But ultimately, after losing sleep on it, it was her anger that triumphed over her fear. No one could just kick her down without a fight. She was a tough cookie to crack, and also more determined now. Yesterday was over. Today she was stronger because of it.

In the subsequent shows, she made sure she danced her absolute best, feeling spurred on by her adversary. She wanted those different roles so badly and was desperate to show Vanya and Boris that she was capable of taking them on. Every time she had asked for a more challenging role, they had said that she wasn't ready, that she was more suited to playing princesses. Zaria would wince but never complain verbally each and every time she heard that. She wished she could play a villain once but knew her sweet face was an impediment to that. The snag was that princesses were beginning to make her feel really, enormously bored. The urge to move outside those roles was stronger than ever, crying out for attention from deep inside her body.

The police investigation of the glass pieces, unfortunately, didn't conclude with a find as there was hardly any evidence to even search for the right person. Zaria was actually glad the drama was over without getting leaked to the media.

After one more year, a door finally opened a crack for her. She was told she would be dancing in the ballet *Flames of Paris* the next season.

"Yes, I think you are ready for different roles now," Vanya said, "Your technique is much more varied after all your work."

Zaria smiled faintly and realised that she felt more calm than excited. It was finally happening. Finally, finally.

Chapter 19

Christmas was just around the corner and Zaria was spending her winter holidays in Moscow this time. Leonid had wanted to take her on a holiday to Spain or the Bahamas on his private jet but she had said she just wanted to spend it at home. The temperatures were freezing and the snow fell heavily outside, with a cloud of fog covering the city. Even so, most Muscovites looked their stylish best with women flaunting their posh footwear and coats. A Christmas tree was lit up in the Red Square, flashing with its multi-coloured lights, exuding the warmth of the festive season. Leonid was taking time off from work for a few weeks so he could spend more time with Zaria. They spent nearly every hour of the day together discussing their lives, their childhoods and their families.

Zaria visited an orphanage one day, where she played and danced with the kids for an hour. The previous year, she had given her monthly pay cheque to the same charity as donation. Doing such meaningful things made her feel good inside, feel grateful for everything she had.

Leonid took her to a very glamorous event one evening—a ball and charity auction which was attended by the elite of Moscow society. The evening was hosted at a billionaire's mansion that was located on the outskirts of the city.

Zaria glanced around the lavish interiors of the humungous mansion that clearly proclaimed that its owner was fabulously rich. The party was on the ground floor, tiled with grey-white marble flooring with the walls painted in matching shades. Tall, large French windows with glass doors opened into the manicured lawns outside, through which she had walked in, in wonder. Scores of people dripping in platinum and diamonds were scattered around the huge hall, sipping drinks and chatting in groups. Some were picking at the wide range of nibbles from the buffet spread out near the wall on the left. To the right, glass doors showed an indoor, heated swimming pool with a tall crystal sculpture of a peacock on one side of it. A huge crystal chandelier hung high above them in the centre of the ceiling, sparkling grandly over everyone at the party.

Zaria chatted with some of Leonid's friends, as they nibbled on caviar and smoked salmon being passed around on plates of gold.

"So we are just back from Paris, where we love to holiday," a woman, who was the wife of one of Leonid's business associates, said. She was dressed in a deluxe green gown, fur coat and emerald earrings. Her face looked botoxed and sculpted and even the rings on her fingers reeked of wealth.

"Oh, I have danced in Paris. It's a lovely place," Zaria replied.

She found it much easier than expected to mix and talk with Leonid's rich set. Some loved ballet and sounded impressed with her being a dancer with the Baranski.

She danced with Leonid in her deep blue designer gown and the diamond choker necklace that he had gifted her. Romantic piano and violin music played from the band that had been hired just for the evening. She smiled at Leonid as she rested her head on his shoulder, and they moved together slowly on the cool, marble floor. Leonid was tall and blonde with a faint stubble and a gentle expression. Zaria thought about him and about where she was. Did she belong here, in this world? Honestly, the answer wasn't coming to her. This part of society was filled with so much wealth, so much so that she felt awkward at certain moments. She wondered what it would be like to be Leonid's wife and whether she would be able to play that role well enough. Would it be possible to balance a marriage with dancing? That seemed a difficult thing to do when she thought about it.

"Are you enjoying yourself dear?" Leonid asked her, his arm firmly around her waist.

"I am, more than I thought I would," Zaria replied.

"Great. And…what do you think of my friends?" Leonid asked, a trifle hesitantly.

"I expected the super rich to be super snobbish. Some really are, but thankfully, not your set," Zaria said, not adding that a few of his friends were talking about diamonds and private planes too much.

Later there was a charity auction, where many items autographed by Russian and other celebrities were auctioned off for different causes. Some items were sold for exorbitant amounts and a jersey belonging to a Brazilian football star went for nearly half a million roubles. Leonid bought a famous Hollywood actor's autographed T-shirt for nearly 100,000 roubles. The proceeds went to a charity for orphaned children which pleased Zaria a great deal.

As they left, she held Leonid's hand in hers as they walked up the road and climbed into his jade green Jaguar. She was sure she hadn't been in love with anyone as much as she was in love with Leonid. He was actually the first man she had fallen truly in love with. He had to be the one. He treated her with a lot of respect and she felt comfortable opening up to him about anything. Most importantly, he respected and understood her career commitments, being a huge ballet patron himself.

They reached their home and Zaria strolled into the plush, deluxe living room with a fluffy, beige carpet. A colossal flat-screen television was stuck to the wall in front of her. Two large, luxurious black couches lined the opposite wall while a white and blue patterned Ming vase was in the centre of the table. A priceless masterpiece by a famous Russian painter hung above the fireplace.

She had moved into Leonid's swanky apartment a few weeks ago, when he had asked her to live in with him. They had been a couple for nearly a year already. He lived in the centre of the city, the most upscale part of town, near where he worked in the business district.

Zaria's cell phone suddenly started ringing, the rock tune she loved blaring out and making her grin. Irina, however, broke some tragic news. Jaya, Zaria's grandmother, had just passed away in Chennai at nearly eighty after battling a heart problem. Zaria listened quietly as her mother spoke words of comfort, urging her to stay strong. Death had to happen, it was inevitable. Irina told her that Jaya had left a large sum of money to Zaria in her will. Zaria felt a tear flow out of her eye. She was now rich thanks to the inheritance, but what was she going to do with so much money? Funny that thought, since she had grown up dying to escape poverty…Now she was living in style with someone rich. She felt some satisfaction in the fact that Jaya had developed a fondness for Irina over the years. She heard Leonid's steps at the doorway and looked up into his eyes.

"What happened darling?" he asked, walking over and sitting down next to her.

She rested her head on his shoulder and started crying. Leonid put his arm around her and stroked her hair. The flames from the fireplace burned and flickered, nestling her in warmth as the snow fell heavily outside.

Zaria had a lovely time during her winter break. She and Leonid spent some time with Irina and Andrei during the Jewish festival of Hanukkah. Her mother had met Leonid before and told her once more that she approved of him very much. Zaria was very happy to hear that since she was serious about him.

Besides that, she was in a phase of her life in her late twenties, where she was feeling more mature, more stable in her career. She felt that she had developed as an artist and improved with time, proving that she could still perform well. God willing, she might even enter a more gratifying place in her career—she was finally getting a chance to dance something different.

Zaria suffered a very serious setback just a few days later. During rehearsal, she was sitting down when two people were moving a heavy, wooden cupboard, a prop, across the room. One mover slipped on a patch of water and lost his grip. The cupboard slipped and crashed down hard on Zaria's left foot. She screamed. The pain spread through her ankle to her entire foot, hitting her like a thunderclap. She heard the movers apologise profusely again and again and heave the prop off her foot with difficulty. The rehearsal director, choreographer and Victor all rushed to her side and asked with concern if she was all right. The excruciating pain shot through every bone and every vein in her foot.

"Aaah…" she groaned, as her face contorted with pain.

She found that she was unable to even stand up. No, she thought. Panic started to rise inside her. Not now, could her foot take another injury?

She found herself in the office of the Baranski's doctor a few minutes later, cursing herself mentally. The grey bearded doctor with thick glasses ran an X-ray on her foot and then examined it closely. Her foot had swollen near the ankle and still hurt terribly. She hoped the injury wasn't critical, it would be the worst time ever to get one.

"Broken bones. And it's a fracture, a really bad one…" the doctor stated plainly, examining a computerised picture on the screen.

Chapter 20

Zaria held her breath. NO NO NO NO NO!

"How long will it take to heal?" she asked very softly.

"This will require surgery, I'm sorry to say. You should have that done by tomorrow morning. Until then a cast for your foot and complete rest. Don't even try to walk. Or you can never get back on stage," the doctor said firmly.

Zaria froze. Was she not going to be able to dance again? She heard the doctor speaking but couldn't process any of the medical terms. Navicular bone, cuneiform. His voice sounded far away, as the impact of her situation fogged her ears.

"So how long will I be out?" She asked, her voice a faint whisper.

"At least five to six months," the doctor stated sombrely.

She was speechless when the bomb exploded. It struck her like a jolt straight from hell. The world stopped. Time stopped. She heard the hum of the air conditioner. It seemed so loud. This had to be a bad dream, a nightmare. But no, it was real. She was awake. She looked down, knowing the tears were starting to pool up in her eyes.

"Thank you, doctor. I'll follow your advice," she said.

Boris didn't give her even a tiny spoonful of sympathy.

"Why did you have to hurt your foot now? You should have been more careful. Now I have to get a replacement for your upcoming show," he reproached her when she told him she couldn't dance for the rest of the season. Zaria thought his attitude was really unfair. Some dancers had taken maternity leave for so many months and he hadn't shown such displeasure towards them. Oh well, she couldn't always be the director's favourite. She didn't want to argue the point with Boris, deciding that keeping quiet was a better option.

Boris made Anastasia replace her immediately in her scheduled ballets. They had both been a hot item for quite some time and rumours amongst the dancers were that they were going to tie the knot very soon. Boris was already creating ballets just for Anastasia and she was able to play him like a puppet. Zaria felt so upset and dismayed at the way that woman was able to virtually get anything she wanted. Where Anastasia was rising higher and higher, she was left stagnating.

Zaria sat on her bed in Leonid's apartment and cursed out loud. She felt so frustrated with herself, though the injury wasn't really her fault. She felt a strong urge to scream or break something. The weeping started, something she was surprised hadn't begun at the doctor's office itself. She cried and cried and cried, sitting there all alone. The sobs made her tremble. Her head hurt and her eyes became red. She didn't know how long she cried, unable to even control her blubbering. She didn't even feel like telling her mother about her injury immediately, but eventually did text her the sad turn of events. Leonid would be at work, but she would call him later. She didn't want him to rush home and see her in this state, so she didn't tell him how serious her injury was. She stared at the splint made of fibre around her left foot, tapping her fingers on the stand next to the bed. Her hand felt cold, and she thought of putting her gloves back on. The Baranski had given her medical insurance and she wouldn't have to pay for the surgery. They also assured her that she would receive her payments since the accident was someone else's fault. Even so, she knew she had suffered a huge loss, one that had torn out a huge piece of her heart. Her left foot had always been weak; she had sprained it more than once in the past. She already knew that though. Why was she repeating that fact to herself again and again?

"If you don't have the surgery you cannot dance again," the doctor had said. She felt so cold when she recalled those words, words that hit her like a deathly blow. Was it the end of her stage life? The thought stared at her like a python from the black pit that stretched below her. She was sure she could lose her mind if she couldn't dance anymore. The one thing she never wanted to happen to her had happened. She couldn't stop it from mowing her down, leaving her broken and bleeding. She picked up a small wooden abstract sculpture from the bedside table. Then she hurled it with all her might. It hit the desk on the other side of the room and fell to the floor with a loud clatter. It didn't break, but rolled across the surface, under the chair and stopped behind the door.

The weather was still bitter, just the way she felt at the moment. She heard the roar of a bike going by outside, jarring her to an ugly fact. She couldn't dance in the upcoming production of *Flames of Paris*. That was a severe kick in the gut, since she had been so earnest to be part of a story set during the time of the French Revolution. She wasn't even sure when she could return to the stage next year, so hasty replacements were being made for her parts in the next season's ballets. What was she going to do during the many months ahead? She couldn't dance. At all. She was stuck.

She picked up the remote and turned on the television. A Russian movie was playing, one that was about a woman who lost her child and then descended into a life of depression. She stared at the screen for an hour but shifted restlessly, not able to keep her focus on the screen. She really needed to talk to one of her friends but the thing was, most of her close friends would be at work now. She logged onto her e-mail and shot off a mail to Tara, Gul and Ashwin about her injury and asked what they were doing. Tara was back in Chennai now and so was Ashwin.

She couldn't stop lambasting her darned bad luck for the hundredth time. Just when she was so eager to do the upcoming show, she had to fracture her foot. Why, why, why did it have to happen? Anastasia was probably gleeful that she was going to be out of action. She thought back to the nightmarish day when she had found the glass pieces in her shoe. That person too would be ecstatic that she'd been knocked down a peg. The gruesome image of the pointed glass and the distress she had tumbled into was something she knew she could never erase. She felt the aggravation build up inside her until she was ready to shriek like a maniac. She stared at the dark patterns on the floor, a spot where she had spilled some coffee, but hadn't cleaned up. She didn't even want to get rid of the stain now. What was the point?

Half an hour later, she was trying to watch a DVD. The movie was a classic Hitchcock one, *The Lady Vanishes.* It was one of her favourites, but she could barely concentrate. Voices came out from the screen, and the sound of the gunshots sounded towards the end of the film as the spy escaped. She felt the pangs of hunger and thought of ordering some food in. She looked at the grey sculpture that stood on one shelf. Its curves were so abstract, almost like you couldn't really understand what they meant.

Picking up her cell phone, she glanced at the message inbox. Leonid had sent her a text asking if she was okay and saying he would be home at six. Igor and Victor had sent her messages asking if she felt better and said they were really sorry about her foot. She thought their messages were really caring, since they must have snuck in the texts during rehearsal when Boris wasn't looking. He never allowed dancers to touch their phones during practice. Ashwin had sent her a very sweet message–'*You hurt your foot? I'm so sorry, hope you get well very soon. I know you were looking forward to your next ballet very much. What are you doing during your injury break? Coming to India by any chance? We can all hang out together. It'll be fun.*'

She smiled when she read it. Ashwin was so thoughtful at times like this. What time would it be in Chennai now anyway? About nine in the morning. Tara would probably be asleep, since she usually slept really late into the day. Gul would be sending off her son Imran to playschool.

She stared at the ceiling while lying on the bed, absent-mindedly looking at the perfectly painted corner, almost too immaculate.

Leonid walked in at around six-thirty.

"I'm really sorry about your foot. Are you all right?" he asked, setting down his briefcase and walking up to Zaria with a very vexed expression. He reached down and hugged her tightly as she remained sitting on the bed. Then he stared at her splint and asked her if her condition was as bad as it looked.

"I can't walk for awhile. I'm really upset. But it will be okay in some months," she lied, hugging him back.

She suddenly didn't feel like discussing her injury and disappointment with him for some reason unknown to herself.

Leonid ordered dinner in for her from her favourite Japanese restaurant and brought everything to her bed on a tray. By the time she had eaten, her mood had become much more cheery. Leonid gave her a kiss and then went to the kitchen to put their plates in the dishwasher. Zaria wasn't sleepy yet so thought of watching TV for a while when Leonid walked back into the room. He walked up to her but didn't sit down and his eyes looked nervous all of a sudden. She smiled at him and was about to ask if anything was wrong when he went down on one knee.

She gasped and watched as Leonid pulled out a small purple velvet box from his coat pocket and opened it to reveal a ring with glittering diamonds in a shimmering circular pattern nestling in it. She stared at the ring. He was proposing to her. And with a diamond ring. The perfect romantic proposal. And he was down on one knee. She started to smile, but startlingly found her mind in a muddle, making her unable to say anything. Why wasn't she saying yes? She had been with him for two years, and she had never been so much in love with any other man before. She had even visualised this moment before, waited for it. She wanted marriage and family at some point in her life and he seemed to be the one. But now, why wasn't she jumping in delight and saying yes? Or laughing and kissing him in ecstasy? She realised she had been looking at the floor for a while and pulled her eyes back to his face. His disappointment at her silence was obvious in his blue eyes. He swallowed and jerked his head down to his hands, lowering the ring. A sudden awkwardness hung between them, something that she had never felt with him since the moment they first met. How long had it been since she had been struck dumb for no apparent reason?

She opened her mouth, but then closed it again.

"Umm…Can I please think about it?" she asked, giving him an apologetic look.

He looked at her but didn't speak. He got to his feet slowly.

"All right. I know you need time to think. You can give me your answer after a while," he said, barely looking her in the eye.

His tone sounded very different. A hint of anger was visible in it. That was a very rare emotion, one that seldom showed its face between them. They had barely fought in all their time together. The last major argument that they had was months ago. He trudged out of the room slowly, his gait reflecting his letdown. She watched him leave and wanted to call out to him. She felt guilt prickle her heavily for not saying yes to him. Had he bought that ring today? Why today? It looked so very expensive. She sat silently for many minutes and tried to understand her feelings, the sudden uncertainty that had sprung in uninvited. How would she able to play the role of a high society wife and be committed to her career as well? The picture just didn't seem to be possible at present. However, she resolved to think hard about the marriage proposal over the next few days. There was time. And even if she wasn't ready for marriage, they wouldn't have to break up. Maybe she wasn't ready for marriage. That must be why she hadn't said yes. That had to be it. Maybe marriage needed to wait a few years.

That night, she and Leonid lay with their backs to each other, not touching and barely speaking. A new feeling of distance was obvious between them, sneaking its way into their relationship.

Zaria went under the surgeon's knife the very next morning. The paranoia about her injury was building up and slowly throttling her. She had a metal disk inserted inside her foot. She wished Leonid could hold her hand through all of it, but he was gone. He had broken up with her and she was still in disbelief over how it had ended. She had told him she didn't want to marry right away, because she didn't feel ready for it. Besides, she had felt she could not balance a career with being a high society wife. But she did not say that aloud to him. He had been disappointed at her refusal and asked her the reason for it, saying that she could continue her career as it was. He then said that it wasn't fair to him because he really wanted to settle down and start a family. She had said that he was overreacting and it led to them having a loud, blazing row that ended terribly. He hadn't known she was going in for surgery the next day. She was sure he wouldn't have argued with her if he had known about it. But she had let the fight happen, something telling her she couldn't stop it even if she wanted to.

She came out after the surgery and the doctors told her that she could get back on stage, but needed to rest for at least five months. No dancing till then. She kept telling herself that until it became meaningless.

She moved in with her mother and Andrei temporarily. She was confined to a wheelchair and was told to not even try to walk for the time being. She needed her mother's help for basic things like having a bath and wearing pants. Andrei, Galya and her mother were extremely supportive. They were like solid rocks and kept insisting that she would surely get back on stage. A doctor visited Zaria regularly to check on her progress and prescribed a list of medications she had to take. Irina gave her all the painkillers, calcium tablets and multivitamins as per the doctor's instructions.

Zaria was sitting in Friendship Park about two months later in her wheelchair, enjoying the evening amidst nature. It was still her chosen favourite spot to reflect in though it was not at all near her flat, unlike when she had grown up. A dainty, crisp breeze blew around her, making strands of her hair fly around her face. The light from the sun shone down on her, the golden rays playing across the green lawn.

She glanced at the many trees that stood nearby, extending high from the ground. The trunks were very tall and thin, greyish and disappearing into the sky. The trees' branches were very lean and hung out like a labyrinth of snakes, woven together yet wild. Leaves on them were sparse and barely visible, in their shades of lime green. The grass flowed on, glistening and thick, yet uneven beneath the wheels of her chair. A road, smooth and long wove through the rows of trees, meandering into the distance. All the colours in the park were of the different hues of nature, blending harmoniously together like a painting. The place was nearly deserted, but she was surprisingly glad to have no one around. A statue of the famous writer Cervantes, the author of *Don Quixote*, stood in the distance, sculpted cleanly in grey stone. Reddish orange flowers grew around it in a circular pattern, symmetrical and neat.

She thought back to her childhood in Moscow, when her mother had taken her more often to Gorky Park as a child. Zaria had loved the rides, mainly the Ferris Wheel which she had wanted to stay on forever.

She had sometimes liked to stay in the park until it grew dark, watching the fountains splash up against the sky until it was time to go home.

She had been advised by the doctor to use a wheelchair for a few months. The seat felt clammy and she felt the discomfort on her backside. A cripple was what she felt like, unable to do anything by herself. She missed Leonid terribly and knew she was still in love with him. He had left her, just walked away despite her pleas. She had cried for a very long time. Gul had sent her a sweet message asking her to come down to Chennai for a while so that she could cheer her up. She had said that Zaria would meet someone else one day and would eventually get over her broken heart. Zaria had also spoken to Ashwin and he had asked if she was feeling better about Leonid and if her foot was healing. She had felt so much better after speaking to him and said she would definitely like to go to Chennai later that year for a few weeks.

On the plus side, she didn't have a marathon daily routine and was free all day. The doctor came home once a week to check her foot and said he would eventually start some basic movement exercises for it. She found time to catch up on the many movies she had missed. Ashwin was really sweet in his e-mails about her injury and Zaria called and spoke to him for two hours one weekend about her breakup, her injury and her depression. After that, they both started talking on Skype for hours quite a few times a month. She felt like she missed him very much.

When no one was watching, she took a quick drag from her cigarette and blew the smoke out slowly, watching the little grey clouds swirl into the air. She'd been smoking much more since her injury and her split from Leonid, to get over her heartbreak. The truth was that she was now a cigarette addict, leaving at least fifteen cigarette stubs in her ashtray every day. Her life seemed to be spiralling downwards in every aspect. She felt caught in a no-win situation, both in her career and her personal life.

She rolled her wheelchair on the narrow pathway past the bright green trees and the low trimmed hedges that bordered the lawn. A statue called "Bread" depicting two naked female figures kneeling on a block, holding a sheaf of wheat between them stood before her. The trees looked sheltering, strong and tall, painted in different shades of green. She wished the radiance and cheerfulness of nature would seep into her and push away the dejection that had caught hold of her in its vice-like grip. Some people who saw her stared at her, pity in their eyes, imagining her to be a cripple. Zaria hated those pitying looks and tried to ignore them.

She wheeled over to where the cars were parked, waiting for Andrei and her mother to come and pick her up. She had insisted that they give her some time alone, assuring them that she could manage by herself for a few hours. She watched the light from the streetlamps throw shadows across the road. The sky was grey and the Moscow skyline with its numerous tall buildings was visible as a pale outline. The heavy Moscow traffic could be heard in the distance, a bustle of angry horns. Ferraris and motorbikes. A drizzle soon began, the drops of rain falling delicately on Zaria's hair. By the time Andrei had driven them all home the rain had started coming down heavily.

Zaria stretched and yawned as she smoked a cigarette from the pack that sat on the couch next to her. She felt she needed to smoke whenever she was stressed out and loved the feel of the cigarette between her fingers. She usually snuck in the extra cigarettes when her mother was out, knowing that her mother would berate her. She glanced at the morning newspaper that was delivered, and as soon as she opened the city page, saw a huge headline with Katya's picture underneath it.

Katya was joining politics. The picture showed her in a long skirt and prim white shirt, standing with several prominent political figures from the city. Oh, great. She was quitting when she was still at the top and grabbing headlines because of it. Zaria scanned the article that said that Katya had accepted an invitation to join the Russian

People's Political Party. At thirty-one, she would be amongst the younger faces of the party that was trying to recruit more women to appeal to the public. Katya was quoted as saying, "I love ballet, but at this stage in my life I feel the need to do more for the people of my country whom I love so much. I will work for…." Yeah, right, Zaria thought. She certainly knew how to stay in the spotlight and now she was going to be a super VVIP.

She tossed the paper down and sighed. Everyone seemed to be hiking up to great heights. As for herself, she felt lost and disoriented. The discomfort in her foot continued, even after the operation. A physiotherapist came home once a week to make her do the smallest of exercises. She hated doing them, wishing that she could leap in the air like she used to. She thought of taking a trip somewhere the next month to clear her mind of its grey clouds of melancholia. She could walk with crutches now, since it was over three months since the surgery. She concluded that the break would be a welcome change of scene. Perhaps she could go to Goa in India. The place was full of Russians and also had great beaches that she had always wanted to see. But she wasn't anywhere near healthy enough to enjoy a holiday like that. Maybe she could do a meditation camp in India, things she had heard so much about. A spiritual retreat would be the perfect thing. It would be okay to go on a trip as long as she didn't exert her foot, the doctor had said. So the trip would be alright then, as long as she didn't walk about too much. By the time her foot was restored to health in the next season, she could actually have more perspective on the current stage of her career and garner her thoughts. Strange, but she was trying to find a tiny positive in her injury.

Zaria went on a trip to the foothills of the Himalayas to be part of a small meditation camp there. Her Indian friend Leela, who was a Kathak dancer, had also joined Zaria, along with some of her friends. Her mother had said she should not travel so soon, but Zaria had been adamant and said that she had the doctor's clearance.

Soon they arrived at a place near the outskirts of Haridwar, one of the most famous spiritual places in India. They met up with ten other people who would also be part of their meditation group conducted by an ashram. Four foreigners were amongst them. A French couple that lived in Pondicherry, near Chennai, was happy to hear Zaria was from Chennai and told her how much they loved the city. They asked Zaria about Russia and her opinion of India from her various visits. She declared that she was in love with India and it was a home away from home for her.

After freshening up at the hotel, they all walked to a grassy area a few minutes from the banks of the river and then sat down in a group to start the meditation. The head of the group was a yoga instructor who headed an ashram. He said that he would be leading them through the meditation.

"Let me start by telling you a little bit about Haridwar and its spiritual significance," he began, before going on to talk about where they were. He told them some facts about the Himalayas too. Zaria knew that the range was home to Mount Everest, the tallest peak in the world, and was between India, China, and a part of Pakistan. She also knew, from the stories her mother had told her during her childhood in Chennai to keep her abreast of both her Indian and Russian cultures, that one of the mountains, Mt Kailash, was, according to Indian mythology, the home of Lord Shiva, one of the three main gods of the believers of Hinduism.

Zaria looked at the scenic beauty of nature spread around her, letting her senses be enveloped and embraced by it. The sky was a clear, pastel blue and the greenery of the trees all around them made her feel rejuvenated even before they began the meditation. The river Ganges flowed with force in the distance, where hundreds of people bathed in its holy waters. They were far away from all that, but could glimpse the flurry of colour and activity of numerous families near the river.

The instructor told them to start with deep breathing. They all sat in a group and obeyed him as he told them to close their eyes first and then start taking slow, deep breaths. Zaria felt the crisp, nippy air around her as she breathed, seated on a stool. Though she couldn't sit cross legged or do any of the yoga exercises with the others she was glad she had come to meditate. She needed to cleanse herself of her doubts and negative thoughts before making her comeback. At the moment dancing on stage again seemed too far away, too blurred to even be near solid. The anxiety had to leave her; the realms of insecurity had to be forgotten. Her spirit needed to gain more strength, more belief, more determination. Being in India made her feel secure and so at home that she knew she would be much happier when she returned to Moscow. The sound of the birds and the activity in the distance was so faint from the peace and stillness they sat amongst. At the end of the session, Zaria felt different, as though her mind was less depressed. She was in a phase of extreme mental turmoil and unhappiness, though she would never admit it to anyone.

On the bus ride back, she and Leela discussed their dance worlds and the shows each wanted to work on next.

Leela then proceeded to start cribbing about one of the top classical dancers in India who according to her was, "dropping her *pallu* and sleeping around all the time." Zaria had to laugh at the way she spoke of it.

Leela went on, "She is always sucking up to the powers that be in Delhi. That is why she gets all the awards."

Zaria gave her a weak laugh, not bursting into her trademark grin. She sympathised with her friend, knowing that she wasn't the only one who had to deal with tussles and ego issues. She felt sleepy and listened as the Indians in the bus indulged in one of their favourite pastimes–politician bashing. Suddenly, she felt her thoughts grow dark as they leaned towards her foot again. The thought of not being able to ever dance again…She could never live like that. She would be as good as dead, a living corpse. Emotions grew heavy, conflicts growing larger by the minute. A tear trickled out of one eye and stained one cheek. She quickly wiped it off and turned her head away. No one had seen it, thankfully.

Zaria stayed with her aunt in Chennai for a whole month. The city was wonderful to be back in, the perfect place where she could sort out her inner battles, with family and friends around her. She was constantly cursing out loud about her injury, and the only funny thing about it was that some family elders insisted that it was because of *dhristi* and evil eyes.

Zaria, Tara, Gul, Ashwin and Farhan were at Amethyst one evening, sipping coffee and munching on potato wedges. They sat on one of the round white marble tables beneath some large, round white lights that hung suspended from the ceiling. This was a place Zaria loved to visit whenever she came to town. A cool breeze blew over from the many potted plants that spurted out from grey brown pots. Tall trees and other plants in various shades of green stood all around the tables in the large, open air space. The floor outside was paved with brown coloured brick and a little pond glistened in a grass patch. The plants were of various shades of light green with some small yellow and pink flowers budding in a few. A small waterfall flowed with a soothing patter on one side of a footpath. Quite a few foreigners were scattered amongst the many people on the tables under the sky, their soft chatter barely ruffling the serene air. The place was soothing and quiet, even amidst the bustling main road traffic outside.

Zaria heard someone at the table laugh, but she just sat on her chair, holding her now stale coffee in her hand and half-listening to her friends' conversation. She noticed a couple sitting together in the nearby table and felt sad. She fiddled with her green hair tie, taking it off and combing out some hair tangles with her fingers. Her cane was propped against her chair, a sore reminder of her foot. She had managed to hobble into the cafe slowly with Ashwin's help.

"Are you okay? I haven't seen you this thoughtful ever," Gul said, putting her arm around Zaria.

"Is it about that guy you almost married?" Ashwin asked from next to her.

"Hey no. She's thinking about her injury guys. Aren't you?" Tara said, looking at Zaria with trepidation.

Zaria tried to smile, but only just managed a very frail one.

"I'm fine, guys. Thanks," she said.

"You said you just had a *feeling* to say no to the proposal, whatever it was," Ashwin said dramatically with his hand on his heart.

"Maybe you're meant to marry another guy," Farhan said. He winked and looked towards Ashwin. Zaria blushed heavily while everyone else laughed.

"Whatever. Don't mention Leonid. I am on holiday, so let's not discuss anything too deep," she said, smiling more with her old friends around her.

Ashwin told her that he was working in his family business in the city now, having just finished his MBA in the UK. Tara, Gul and Farhan were in deep conversation about Devinder's hilarious joke forwards on e-mail.

"Earth calling the ballet princess. Hello?" a voice rang out, cutting through Zaria's thoughts. It was Ashwin's.

Zaria realised that he had been talking to her about something for a whole minute, but she had been completely tuned out.

"Hey, don't worry. I'm sure you are going to come back better than ever," Ashwin said, giving her arm a squeeze. Zaria smiled back. A faint one, but she did.

Her friends took her shopping and after a month of being with them she felt her depression fading away. Her chirpiness slowly returned and she felt more certain of her comeback. She felt deep inside that the trip to India had helped her gain insight into herself. The holiday had lifted her spirits and she felt better. She knew getting her confidence back would be a gradual process and not an overnight one. Importantly, she understood clearly that her mind and body still wanted to dance. She wanted to, even if her injury was nearly fatal to her stage career. Even if she missed out on precious time and had to start from a step behind again. She had to get back on stage, she felt so incomplete and naked without her tutu on. She was literally counting down the days on a calendar until the day the doctors said she could try and walk without a cane.

The whole injury episode had actually made her more of an adult, made her appreciate what she had more. She prayed everyday that her foot would heal so that she could dance again. Being a positive thinker, she felt that it would happen. The doctors had said it would if she listened to them, hadn't they? So why should it not happen? Yes, it would, and she would set the stage on fire yet again with her scintillating performances.

Chapter 21

Unfortunately for Zaria, her foot didn't heal fully in the anticipated six months and her comeback had to be postponed. The doctors cut open her foot again and removed the metal disk. It was more than a month later than anticipated when they allowed her to go back on stage. And then came the day she was waiting for. Finally.

The curtains drew apart slowly and the lights lit up the sets once more. Zaria felt the stage beneath her feet again and sighed the minute she was on it. An invisible one, but still there. She felt like the power to enchant, to mesmerise had been stolen from her. Her feet performed every step carefully, caressing the stage surface as her shoes touched it once more. She wasn't sure of remembering all the steps as they had rehearsed in just a month. Her limbs felt distinctly more unsure than they used to be, as they moved after a long hiatus. When she raised her leg high the muscles felt tight, as though she had to unlock them all over again. Her body didn't feel as strong or as confident in its movements as it used to. Ten minutes into the show, her foot felt a twinge. But nothing more. Her fears vanished after the First Act. The stage was so large, so much larger than she remembered it.

The Acts rushed by and the show reached its conclusion. Zaria held hands with Victor and bowed. Loud cheers echoed through the auditorium. A steady stream of clapping hands was seen in the audience, like a wave that rose and fell all around. The crimson red seats were filled to capacity, she realised as her eyes took in the spectators. So many people. So many applauses. A shower of long stemmed red roses was flung onto the stage at Zaria's feet, the grandest ovation for a ballerina. She knelt down and broke into her trademark bright smile. She was really here. She was back. Amazing. It seemed like only yesterday when she thought she could never get back on stage. Tears brimmed over from her eyes. She didn't blink them away.

Life was beautiful.

Her time away had made her resolve firmer, since she understood how integral ballet was to her being. She could never live without it. Dancing again helped her out of the personal depression she'd been in for the past few months. She'd also controlled her smoking addiction, smoking only occasionally now much like her pre-depressive phase.

The comeback shows in spring made her confidence and gaiety return, amidst new challenges. She also wanted to stay at the level of finesse needed of her, so that she could hang on to principal parts and not be shoved away in favour of younger faces. She worked out more, ensured her body was fit and started using more beauty products to keep herself looking young. More facials and pedicures became the norm, something she hated doing when she was younger. Another bomb didn't go off when she was contracted until the end of the year. The heads of the Baranski felt that she still had the beauty and ability that some younger dancers didn't. Thank goodness they hadn't said she was nearing thirty and packed her off. But the need to live up to

Boris' expectations mounted as he was constantly opting for younger dancers over the more experienced ones.

One day at rehearsal, Zaria was sitting down on the hard benches, sipping her energy drink. She watched Anastasia go and sit next to Boris while he sipped some water. She leaned very close to him, put her arm around his waist and murmured into his ear. Boris looked completely infatuated, as he too slipped his arm around her and his cheeks flushed crimson.

"I bet they are going to walk down the aisle soon," Victor whispered to Zaria.

Zaria simply nodded. She watched Anastasia and felt her envy at not being where she was. Boris was already treating her as the main star of the group and Zaria could barely come to terms with it. She had just asked Boris and Vanya that day if she could try dancing a contemporary ballet, since the Baranski was just starting to stage more of those.

"*Nyet*, your technique is not ready for that yet, we told you," Boris had said curtly.

Zaria couldn't forget his tone, the seeming dooming finality of his words. She realised that she would never move past where she was, would never be able to move outside the princess roles that she was stuck in. She watched Boris and Anastasia kiss and felt more depressed than she had ever been in months. Even though she was back on stage all her former euphoria vanished in a jiffy on hearing Boris's harsh verdict.

On the bright side, the Baranski was touring America that summer and she was part of the troupe.

Zaria walked on the pavements glancing up at the looming skyscrapers that disappeared into the clouds. The bright neon signs, large billboards, bustling mob of vehicles and sound of horns from the yellow taxis made her enjoy Manhattan more than any place she had visited. So much energy in the air, she thought. The city felt so exhilarating in its enormity and was a melting pot of so many cultures, besides being a shopper's paradise. The other dancers were tired from the morning's rehearsal and said they needed to rest but Zaria had decided to walk around the city. She had found it amusing when the few Americans they had met since they landed had remarked on how her English was so good. She would always respond with "I grew up in India!" and she'd sometimes add that Indians spoke better English than the Americans. That made them smile with her.

She walked amongst the business-like people in their suits and skirts, some pushing baby strollers. The smell of hot dogs from a stand she passed wafted over. She passed a pizza joint and drooled at the delectable looking large slices on display, but she knew she had to be careful about her weight. She thought she must look like a summer beach bum with her capri pants, sleeveless tank top, sandals and sunglasses.

She was strolling along Fifth Avenue, glancing into every single store window she passed. Window shopping, being amongst the high-end designer stores, gave her a girlish thrill. She gawked at the labels like Louis Vuitton, Prada, Gucci, Versace and Cartier that all had their stores on the street. While she was admiring a red and mauve dress on a mannequin in the window, someone walked into her hard, head first. She cried out in pain, her hand flying to her forehead. Her sunglasses clattered onto the pavement.

"I'm so sorry ma'am, are you all right?" a familiar voice said, full of concern.

She whipped her head up in surprise and saw Ashwin. It was really him! They both looked at each other for a moment before bursting into laughter.

"What are you doing here?" she said, grinning and giving him a hug. His cologne smelt so good, she thought. He wore a navy blue T-shirt and jeans and took his sunglasses off to talk to her.

"Oh, I'm just passing through here on a trip to California to visit a cousin of mine," he said with a wide grin. "I didn't know you would be here. Performing?"

He looked very surprised yet glad to have run into her.

"Yeah. But this is such an um, nice coincidence to bump into you," Zaria said, fidgeting with her handbag strap and hoping she wasn't blushing.

They made plans to meet for dinner that evening, to catch up before Ashwin left the city. As Zaria walked on, she was still thinking about their unexpected meeting. It was complicated to figure out how she felt about him. They were now close friends. Over the past few years they had even discussed their current beaus with each other. She also did have romantic feelings for him, but they were too far away so she didn't speak of them.

That evening, she walked into the Spanish tapas bar at half past seven in her black pants and silky aqua top. She hoped that she looked all right. Why was she suddenly so self-conscious anyway? She spotted Ashwin sitting at a table near the bar and waved to him.

"Hello. I'm on time, right?" she said, with a grin, walking up to him, a wide grin lighting up her face.

He got up and said, "Oh hey! You look great. You are not late, I was just a bit early, that's all. "

She sat across from him and saw that his eyes kept flitting to the TV screen above his head. The sound of commentary was faint, amidst the music playing above it.

She rolled her eyes and said, "Oh, no. Not another football match?"

"Umm, hmm" he said, looking back at her. "I'm not really watching. Tell me, what's up with you?"

They sat at a round table by the window amidst the dense New York crowd that filled the place. Many young people sat in groups, some talking noisily on the round booths that stood around the bar. Some attractive women in short skirts and skimpy tops littered the table at the counter. Behind that was an enormous bar, which was stocked with a wide variety of wine and spirits. Some people were still in suits, ties and work clothes, trying to unwind. The room was very dimly lit and the sound of people chatting lent a hum to the air that mixed with the loud disco music playing.

"Oh, been so busy with a new show and touring…the usual. What about you. What's new from Chennai?"she asked.

She couldn't help noticing how his dark hair looked so sexy curled under his ears. They talked through their dinner about his work in Chennai and what their other friends in India were doing. She also told him everything about what she had been up to in Moscow and her ballet life. She found herself completely at ease with him, being able to talk about anything and everything. He could make her laugh easily when he sensed that she was down. When she told him she felt frustrated with Boris' special treatment towards Anastasia, he made jokes about Boris that made her laugh and forget those worries instantly. She noticed she was suddenly very conscious when they touched, even if she was just punching him on the shoulder. The tapas snacks were delectable from the grilled cottage cheese ones to the ratatouille and crepes. Ashwin ordered four different kinds and she tasted them all, while being aware of her growing attraction for her friend.

After an hour, she said she felt like an iced tea since she wanted to chat for a while longer. As they both sat sipping their drinks, she found her thoughts turn towards a major, confusing decision she had to make.

"What are you thinking so seriously about? Hello?" Ashwin joked, making her look up from her drink.

"Oh, it's just…I haven't told anyone except my mother this, okay?" she whispered, making Ashwin lean forwards a little.

"I've been asked to join the Stuttgart Ballet. They're offering me more money, and Alexandr, who's the director there says he will help me work towards doing some abstract ballet–things that I want to do," she said.

"So you don't know if you should take it or not?" he asked, reading her thoughts.

"Yeah…" She said, swirling her straw in her drink. "I don't know if my contract at the Baranski will get renewed after this season. If it doesn't, I will have to retire early…" she said softly, her eyebrows furrowing, her expression grave.

"So from what you say, the Stuttgart offer sounds good. Maybe you should take it," he said.

"It's not that easy to decide!" she snapped, her tone sounding angry when she hadn't intended it.

"Hey, sorry. You're the one who keeps complaining about this Boris dude and you asked for my advice," he said, taken aback.

"I wasn't complaining about him so much. It's the roles," she said, once again letting her anger out unconsciously. She immediately regretted it and felt her cheeks start to heat up. Why was she letting him see her inner frustrations anyway? It wasn't his fault that she was in a dilemma.

"Okay!" Ashwin said, throwing his hands up. "I was only trying to help."

"Look, I'm sorry. I'm just confused. I shouldn't have gotten upset," she said, looking at him apologetically and placing a hand on his shoulder.

"Hey, chill. No problem. I know you are under a lot of pressure," he said, cutting her short. He patted her hand and got a smile out of her.

They sat and talked for a few minutes more, about Gul's joy in motherhood and about Farhan being forced to babysit for his nephew on a few occasions. Zaria glanced at her watch and was very disappointed to realise how time had shot by so swiftly.

"Hey, I have to be up early so I think I should be getting back. I'd love to talk longer but…" she trailed off.

"Hey, it's cool. I understand," Ashwin said, signalling to a waiter for the bill.

He paid the whole bill despite her protests and then offered to walk her back to her hotel. She couldn't refuse and neither did she want to. He was being gentlemanly, even holding the door open for her. He put his arm around her shoulders as they walked together slowly along the pavement. Zaria was acutely aware of the chemistry between them, the romantic tension that was very much there. When they reached her hotel, she turned to him and thanked him before giving him another hug. He gave her a kiss on the cheek and said goodnight. She waved to him as he walked away from her and finally strolled into the lobby. The lavish interiors and bright lighting hit her hard from the darkness outside and she had to blink.

She was just sitting on one of the couches in the lobby to rest her feet when she saw Ashwin returning. Did he forget something? She got up and remained standing, her eyes locked on him as he walked in and spotted her.

"I wanted to ask you something," he said, sitting her down. His voice suddenly sounded different, more serious. He ran his hand through his thick hair and sucked in a breath, before looking straight into her eyes. His eyes looked so dark, so mysterious, so familiar. She caught herself staring into them and tried to sit up straighter. How she wanted him to kiss her. She was very close to him on the beige sofa, his jeans brushing her knee. His eyes were drawing her closer and closer. And then they were kissing before she knew it. She was responding with fervour, delight, everything in the moment.

She woke up, rubbed her eyelids and then sat up, propping up her pillow behind her. Then she froze as she remembered what had happened the previous night. It had been amazing, erotic, sexy, and… reckless? No, it was just a very spontaneous moment she didn't regret in the least. That, she was a hundred percent certain of. She then saw Ashwin staring at her from the chair to the right, wearing just his navy blue boxers. She found herself glancing at his chest and felt her cheeks grow hot. She was glad she was wearing her shirt, though it was a flimsy one.

"Sorry, I'll leave if you want to change," Ashwin said, getting up and walking to the bathroom.

She mumbled a barely audible thank you, flushing again. Her clothes and underwear were scattered around the room and she retrieved them and got dressed. Then she remained sitting on the bed, her feet grazing the soft, velvet carpet. She stared at the bathroom door for a few minutes, wondering what to say to Ashwin about what they had done. An impulsive night, that was all, they wouldn't have to discuss it. She again remembered the feel of his body against hers, on top of hers.

Ashwin walked out from the bathroom fully dressed and stood a few feet in front of her. Zaria kept her eyes on the floor but they drifted to his dark feet. He cleared his throat and her head shot up.

"Okay. I want to ask you something…" he said, his face looking like he was about to grin, but not quite.

She looked at him with curious eyes, her mouth about to open in protest. She had hoped he wouldn't want to discuss what had happened, last night.

"Will you marry me?" he said.

Zaria gasped out aloud and gaped at him. He was serious.

"Is this some kind of a joke? No I'm sorry. You're serious," she said slowly, her voice catching. Her lips curved upwards into a soft smile as she looked into his dark eyes. They had a fire and an intensity she hadn't seen before.

The silence wasn't uncomfortable at all, but felt like it was barely there, just the amount needed. Her thoughts started rushing so fast, she was sure her pulse was starting to quicken. She didn't know what to say, how to put her feelings for him into words. She looked at him and saw his eyes glint with amusement at her incomprehension.

"Well, you know I like you that much," he said. He chuckled and she knew that he was telling her what she already knew. He had liked her for so many years. Now they had become so very close and she was sure she liked him too. A lot. Maybe she loved him, but didn't realise it. Or she did but didn't want to say it because there wasn't a realistic chance of them having a relationship across continents.

"You know, if it wasn't for my ballet now…" she said, "I might have said yes. But I'm still dancing so…"

"I know that. But what if your contract doesn't get renewed?" Ashwin said, his face clearly frustrated.

But there was a barrier that Zaria couldn't break through, however many times she hit it. She wanted to remain active in dance for some more time, some more years. She couldn't say yes to him. Not now.

"I don't want to marry now. I want to dance for a few more years," she said, her tone firm.

"Okay, I know that…But what if your contract doesn't…" he started. "Can't you dance in India?" he asked, knowing the answer.

"No," he answered himself.

"No. Ballet doesn't have much scope there," she said, slowly.

He didn't want to give up. He walked up to her and took her hands in his own.

"Why not marry me? I'll give you everything you need and we will live our lives together," he persisted.

She felt that this meant that he didn't seem to understand her ambitions. She flung his hands away and let the hot anger pour out of her.

"You think I am interested in your money? I'm not one of those girls. You have to get it. My ballet comes first and I can't give it up for anything. So I can't marry you….Right now my career is at its peak…and I've got so many more years left to dance…And, though it's so sweet that you proposed, I mean…Look…I'm sorry, I didn't mean to yell, but…I'm sorry I have to say no to you… It's hard for me too…so confusing…Look, what happened with us last night, it was so…you know…reckless, I mean…yes, it was that although… well… I don't want to discuss it right now…please. Although I need time to think…How do I feel about you? It's so hard for me, since you're so far away. I'm just so confused to talk clearly right now… I don't know…I mean, I do have feelings for you and that makes it so complicated for us both now…and its hard…And my dancing… It would be so much simpler if we were in the same place really."

The words slipped out, seeming to speak themselves before she could even shape them correctly.

"Zaria, wait. I know how much your ballet means to you…," Ashwin said gently.

She went on. "Well, then you should understand that I want to dance now," she said.

"I asked you because my parents think I should get married soon or start meeting girls for that…I thought of you first," he said, looking straight at her.

She was still upset at herself for her anger, for taking it out on him when it was actually not even his fault.

"Oh…It's so sweet that you asked me…," she said, feeling flattered that he had. That was the truth.

"It's okay. I get your situation," Ashwin said, his face looking dejected and crestfallen.

He said goodbye to her, saying he understood and that they were still good friends. He said that he had to leave on the afternoon flight to California.

Then he turned around and left, walking away from her and closing the door before she could even say goodbye properly.

After her rehearsal that morning, Zaria went back to her room after eating lunch. She didn't want to talk to any of her best friends about her very personal feelings regarding Ashwin. She needed to think for awhile, by herself, to let her thoughts become clearer. She had gotten a missed call and a message from Tara hours ago but she hadn't replied yet. Ashwin must have told his friends that he had proposed. Great. She knew Tara could read her easily and knew just how much she liked Ashwin. So now the whole of Chennai would know what had happened, knowing the way gossip travelled fast. She messaged Tara and Gul back saying, "I don't want to talk about it now. I'll tell you both later."

She would call and tell them the whole story later, once the shows in New York were done. Today, she had to think about the show and not get sidetracked from it.

She had always known that she would never cut short her career for marriage. The proposal had admittedly taken her by surprise.

Ashwin was still in love with her. That was so sweet. Was he the one? Maybe he was. She knew for certain that she was strongly attracted to him and wouldn't forget the night they had shared. But the timing was wrong. She wanted to keep dancing and if her contract didn't get renewed, she could take up the Stuttgart offer. Yes, the stage still had magic for her. She still loved the dancing, the touring and the applause. If she had stopped enjoying it she would have stopped dancing years ago. But she still felt that thrill for the stage when she twirled and as long as that flame burnt, she wanted to dance. Until the spark faded. Until thirty at least. Or a year after that.

Otherwise she would have said yes to Ashwin. Definitely, it would be great to spend the rest of her life with someone like him. She was now certain that she was in love with him too, but they were so far apart it was infuriating.

The Baranski's piece was showcased at the iconic Metropolitan Opera House and was a huge success. Zaria had a swarm of things thrown at her feet. Besides flowers she was thrown men's underwear, T-shirts, scarves, men's hats and even phone numbers scrawled on scraps of paper. She laughed as she picked some things up, feeling like a Rockstar.

Afterwards, Igor snapped pictures backstage with all the Baranski people present. It was his last show. He was thirty-five and said his body needed a rest from the stage. He was going to retire to teach at a ballet school in St Petersburg. Zaria told him she would miss his presence sorely, especially on tours. He had become one of her closest friends over the years.

"I will still be in Russia so I am just a phone call away," Igor said as he, Zaria and Victor posed for a snapshot together. As Zaria grinned for the camera, she wondered how she would feel when she danced for the last ever time. Right then she didn't want that moment to arrive, hoping that her body wouldn't wear itself down.

The whole group had a celebratory gathering in Boris' suite at night. Zaria got really drunk and had a great time making a fool of herself as did the others.

She was back in her hotel room afterwards, her head on the spongy pillow. She tried to sleep but was not able to do so for a while.

The e-mail from Alexandr had come so unexpectedly, fallen into her hands out of nowhere. When she'd read it, she stared at it for what must have been a whole minute. It seemed like it was the ideal answer to her agonies. Alexandr had asked her to join the Stuttgart Ballet, for which he was the head honcho. He said that he understood that she wanted to do different ballets, that he would help her towards that goal. Zaria had been quite upset after her rehearsal that very day. She'd heard that Anastasia and Boris were getting married soon. Boris was too wrapped up in Anastasia to ever let her, Zaria, move forwards. She'd finished practice thinking that she'd never move clear of where she was at the Baranski. She continued to feel unfulfilled as a ballerina, knowing something was lacking. She'd even cried over this conflict more than once in the past. A huge boulder was blocking her path, a boulder she could never move. And then the e-mail came and changed everything. It seemed like a fairy with a wand was in front of her, coming out of nowhere, ready to grant her a wish.

An hour passed as she thought long and hard, seriously pondering the choice she was faced with. Finally, she arrived at a decision. She needed a change. The move to Germany would be really good for her. Alexandr was a close friend and he would personally help her career move forwards. He liked her dancing, he knew she had been injured and said that he wanted her to regain her lost time. He said he would try to let her eventually do some contemporary or neoclassical ballets too. The offer was so good. She didn't understand why she hadn't made her mind up earlier. She would get better pay, be in a new country and find more contentment in her dancing too. She had been in Moscow for so many years. A move somewhere else would be refreshing. One of her friends who danced in Stuttgart for some years said it had been a lot of fun. She could have a whole new experience.

She listened to the low hum of the air conditioner. She felt calmer now, after finally arriving at her decision. She needed that novelty and freshness. The time was ripe for a change, perfect even. Stuttgart would be the best. She would e-mail Alexandr first thing the next morning.

Chapter 22

After her twenty-eighth birthday, Zaria found herself in a place she never thought she would be in. She wasn't in Stuttgart but was still in Moscow, her beloved Moscow. Her contract with the Baranski had been renewed for another two years, much to her relief. Only Victor had known that she was thinking of leaving but word must have leaked out because the heads had begged her to stay and had given her a more lucrative contract. She was pleased on knowing that they considered her such a valuable dancer. She had also thought that starting as a girl in the corps de ballet (one of the dancers in the chorus) again in Stuttgart, as per their rules, would have been a backward step. Yes, that would have been a huge risk to take even if it was guaranteed that she could move up quickly. Her body wasn't as fit as years ago, and she had a very slim chance of rising up all over again with a new group. She wanted to continue her principal dancer status in the last stage of her career. Her head had finally told her that she should appreciate what she had, which gave her more insight. The constant internal whining over the years of not being able to do the parts she wanted now sounded childish. She felt guilty about it and realised that she was extremely fortunate to even be where she was. In the end it wasn't the money that prompted her decision. It was her heart. The Baranski was much more renowned than the group in Germany and she had worked her way up there, something she might not be able to do all over again given her age. Also, chance to dance in a different kind of ballet was not far away, from what Vanya had been hinting at. So she had changed her mind at the last minute and told Alexandr that she wasn't going to accept his offer just a day after she had been so sure. That was her. Ever changing, going with the flow.

She didn't feel a wave of gloom sweep over her in her last phase of dancing like Igor had predicted. She remembered all the tours to exotic countries she had been a part of. The Baranski had made it possible for her to see Germany, Austria, Spain and Italy. As a little girl, she could only dream wistfully of visiting such places from the picture books she would thumb through. Now, each country she visited she learnt a few words of a new language. Newness was always fun for her. She felt that ballet had given her a lifestyle so different from the one she had growing up, given her fulfilment, exploration and so much more. But there was a part of her that was looking forward to life after dancing. She was still so young and when her career ended, she would have a long life ahead of her to live and experience. After she hung up her pointe shoes, she didn't want to do anything like choreography, but wanted to be far away from ballet for some time. The next phase of her life would be more relaxed and she actually found herself looking forward to it. She didn't know where she would be then, in Russia or outside. Tomorrow was another day.

She was thrown when she heard one day that Ashwin might be getting engaged. The jealousy bubbled up from inside her, screaming out its protests vehemently. Why? She had said no to him and it wasn't fair to start being possessive. The girl he was getting engaged to was a well-educated one from Bangalore called Aditi. Zaria knew that Aditi was his second choice, that she was the one he actually wanted. Though she had rejected his proposal, she felt resentful about Ashwin marrying someone else. She remembered the short period during which they had dated in the Chennai monsoons. The time when he hadn't wanted to go on a big date because there was a huge cricket match on. His cricket fanaticism had been so cute to her. Anyway, thinking about him now didn't make any sense at all. She still had feelings for him, but there was just no point dwelling on them too much. Everyone had their own lives to lead.

The Baranski was doing some shows in Italy on a tour and Zaria was part of the group that performed in Rome. She saw the Colosseum, the fabulous fashions and tasted raw snails. Her partner fell ill and she danced with a last-minute replacement that she could barely coordinate with. She laughed to herself at some guys backstage who flirted with the ballerinas like they were call girls. Also, the stage was a little hard and she nearly hurt her left foot again but taped it and went on. At times like these, she missed Alexandr sorely. He would always reassure dancers if they felt weak before a show, personally pep them up. Boris never did that. When they returned to Moscow, Zaria willed herself to forget being in the twilight of her stage days and just live in the moment. Her body was still willing and able to take the shows, not yet telling her that it wanted to stop. Knowing that she was in the last stretch of her career made her enjoy every show more. Shocking, to say the least. She had always thought she would be the one who cried when she performed for the last time.

Irina was now involved in a single mother's charity in Moscow and wanted to do the same in India as well. Zaria wanted to help her mother in the cause since her mother's story had made her really feel for single mothers everywhere. That December, she travelled to Chennai with her mother and Andrei to meet social workers. She was doing only two ballets that year and the next, not wanting to tire herself out.

"I'm glad I finally got to visit Chennai. Irina has told me so much about this city," Andrei said, as the three of them walked on the beach after an evening snack at a nearby restaurant.

They all strolled slowly on the soft sand, not minding it getting all over their dressy shoes. Zaria watched her mother chatter—about the places she would show Andrei and about all the things Indian that she wanted to tell him more about. In her fifties, Irina still looked just as gorgeous as she had ten years earlier. The grace in her face was enhanced by a newfound personal calmness she said she had found.

"I told him how much I love Chennai and now he loves it too. I hope we can retire here," Irina whispered to her daughter.

Zaria found herself wanting to agree with her mother's words. Somehow, she did want to come back to India in a way, hoping that something would draw her back years later. Then her mind turned to something else, something she was trying hard to avoid thinking about. From the word going around, people couldn't understand why she had said no to Ashwin's proposal. Zaria was sure the whole of Chennai society was gossiping about it since some knew that he had been after her for years. According to what she heard, some people were saying, "Well, her career is almost over apparently, she can marry him and live like a millionaire. Why did she say no?"

Zaria felt both annoyed and misunderstood at their talk. She wanted to keep dancing for now. And she intended to continue until her body could take it. She had said no to Ashwin nicely after all, and they were still good friends. She didn't understand the narrow-mindedness of Indians regarding marriage and wished they would understand that her dreams were not something she would give up just like that. She needed to live out this stage in her life and have her own sense of when she wanted to stop. She liked being seen as an independent woman, who could stand on her own feet. It was the feminist trait that she had inherited from her mother. And the bottomline was that she loved being a ballerina too much to stop suddenly.

She walked on the soft sand, the cool ocean breeze whipping strands of hair into her eyes. She pushed them away with one hand as she walked up to the water, her long skirt blowing against her legs. Her mother and Andrei were walking together a short distance away, engrossed in conversation. Tuning their voices out, she stood and watched the waves as they crashed and flowed back. The sound was so rhythmic, like music that could make all worries fade away.

She slipped her shoes off and walked closer to the water. The sea water was almost cold, as it lapped at her feet gently. She remembered playing on the beach as a little girl, how she had loved building sandcastles and splashing in the water. The sun was setting, the orange orb in the distance dipping lower over the water. A reddish mane of light glowed around the sun, like a ring of fire. The blaze spread into the surrounding sky in strands of orange amidst the growing darkness. She watched the black outline of birds as they flew in the sky, over the water where ripples of the night were appearing. Shafts of light from the setting sun cut through the dark surface of water, lighting up parts of the waves. The sea was deep and endless, flowing for miles along the coast. Chennai held so many fond memories for her, her happiest childhood days had been right here. The city had a special place in her heart and it was so unique. The warmth of Indians, the colourful culture, the lovely family she had here all made it so. She hoped she could somehow stay close to India, to visit when she wanted, when her dancing days were over. She didn't know where she would be then, where life would take her. Perhaps she would be in Russia or somewhere far away. In India maybe? She would follow her spirit, wherever it chose to run to, wherever it led.

Back in Moscow, she was soon rehearsing again, preparing for her next show. She had her feet massaged often by the Baranski's masseuse, never wanting to hurt them again. The drive to excel on stage was still very much embedded in her. But when she thought of her last bow, she found herself sometimes looking forward to the next chapter in her life, a more leisurely one.

One Monday, she finally received a chance to grab hold of an object that she had been waiting for, for years.

"You can try dancing in a contemporary ballet we are going to put up next season," Boris said to her during rehearsal.

Zaria was struck speechless. Boris playfully slapped her face to make her talk again after nearly ten seconds.

"Boris, can I kiss you for this? I really want to!" Zaria squealed, her eyes shining as she jumped up and down. Boris gave her a pat on the back and walked off to look over the notes with the rehearsal director leaving her looking ecstatic.

Zaria was astonished and felt like all the air had been knocked out of her. Though she had known the day was not far off, she hadn't expected to get the chance today of all days. She had been told the style of dancing was not one she was ready for, no matter how many times she had asked Boris and Vanya to let her try it. Her technique hadn't been good enough for the change according to them. Whenever she had asked over the past few years Vanya would always say, "You're not ready yet."

She had then accepted that she would never be able to do one. But now things had changed again. In her exhilaration, she did a series of cartwheels on the rehearsal floor. The other dancers all cheered and clapped at her enthusiasm and Zaria bowed dramatically.

Boris came back to her and said, "Well, Vanya said you asked her earnestly about this before and after a lot of talking we decided that you can do it. *Da,* I trust Vanya's judgement and think you are ready for this," he finished, patting her on the back.

Zaria had a wide smile stuck on her face now, showing all her teeth. She was finally getting her chance. And no way would she hurt her foot again. She grinned all through that day's rehearsal, prompting Vanya to remark on it.

Chapter 23

The next summer she was part of another exotic tour to London where the group danced at the Royal Ballet Theatre. London was bustling and lively and she hung out with Victor as they saw Piccadilly, Westminster Abbey and strolled around Harrods. Two of the dancers in the corps found their tutus had been misplaced and danced with temporary replacements that were borrowed. Zaria danced after getting blisters just the previous day, with strips of one-inch adhesive tape on parts of her feet. She was finally doing one or two contemporary ballets, after thinking she would never reach that goal. When she thought of goals she thought of Sasha the joker who had actually succeeded in getting into Guinness Book for wearing the maximum number of T-shirts—two hundred and sixty! Two days ago, Zaria read in the paper that Edward had briefly been detained by the police after singing on a busy main street wearing a wig and a cocktail dress—

Sasha's bet! However, Edward was a lawyer and had argued that there was no law against singing in public or against him wearing the dress that he sported. The police had let him off after some yelling. Zaria had giggled as she read the news snippet. The whole thing was so damn funny.

Zaria walked on the concrete pavement, the people around her a mixture of characters, shapes and sizes. Petite women, men who were bulky, short, tall; different faces with varied expressions of their day in their eyes—frustration, anger and contentment strolled around her. Children's voices mixed with old ones called out in the evening, the Russian words giving her a sense of belonging. She pulled her coat tighter over her and put on the last few buttons, the thick coat fitting her snugly. The air of autumn was nippy, making her feel thankful her toes were in her shoes. She walked past the glitzy stores, noticing the wide range of dresses on display. A couple walked arm in arm in front of her, obviously smitten. A little boy who looked no more than seven was begging at the end of the street corner. His face looked frail and frozen, she observed, as he held out a shabby hat with holes. Zaria felt her heart wrench as she dipped into her pocket to give him a rouble. The child's eyes lit up as he murmured a thank you and gave her an endearing smile. She smiled back and then waved goodbye to him as she walked along.

Touring had always been one of her favourite parts of dancing but these days Zaria didn't enjoy it as much as she normally did. Tucked away in the back of her mind was a feeling she couldn't quite understand. The day wasn't that far off, but when she thought of it she found herself imagining an emptiness, a meaninglessness to her life, without ballet. She was going with the tide as usual, and didn't want to start planning the life she would lead after her last curtain call. The image of her pointe shoes gathering dust was agonising to think about, even unbearable at times. At other times, she imagined a relaxed life, without constant rehearsals. How would she deal with it, the transition in her life then? Would it happen too soon, too suddenly, when she wasn't prepared for it? She smirked as she expelled those serious thoughts away. She would be like she always had been. Enjoy today, forget tomorrow. Change was always fun, after all.

Zaria found herself in Chennai that December, once again in her second home. She hung out with her friends as much as she could and they had a blast partying together. The weekend arrived quickly and Ashwin was having a party at his beach house.

Tara's deep green Jaguar pulled into the driveway of the beach house on East Coast Road. The house was a really large one with a red tiled roof and cream coloured walls. A huge lawn was in front, where many people sat sipping drinks and chatting. The beach was very near the house, only a few minutes walk. They all got out of the car and started walking towards the house, Tara stumbling in her high heels. As Zaria walked in through the gate and across the lawn, many people turned to her and said hello. She smiled and hugged friends she hadn't seen in a very, very long time. Tara, Gul and Zaria hung together and chatted with some classmates who had returned to the city after years.

"It looks like everyone is married now," Zaria joked as she stood holding her glass of vodka.

"Yeah girl," said Tara, laughing. "It seems like we are one of the few who aren't. Personally, I don't think marriage is for me though my parents…"

Zaria sat down on a bench nearby, and continued to catch up with her friends. She was clad in a skimpy white spaghetti strap top and black pants with a pair of dangling earrings as her only adornment or accessory. Casual and charming. Just what she was aiming for. Her shoes rested on the green lawn, the blades of grass a little prickly yet smooth. Time seemed to have flown by so fast, from the time they had all been toddlers in school. Tara and Gul went off to dance but she didn't join them, saying she wanted to finish her drink first. The mix of orange juice and vodka she was sipping was tangy and she wondered why she didn't feel the urge to get completely drunk like years before. She felt suddenly self conscious and didn't feel like dancing to the foot-tapping party tunes the DJ was playing on the dance floor. She knew Tara and Gul would understand her sudden abnormal mood. Not wanting to be right in the middle of the party was very odd but wanting to be alone with her thoughts was something that was happening more and more often, she noticed. Maybe she was letting go of the child inside her slowly, without realising it.

Ashwin suddenly popped up in front of her and waved his hand in front of her eyes.

"Hello…Aren't you going to come and dance?" he said in a sing-song voice. "Or is my party boring?" he continued, in an amused tone. Zaria noticed he wore a black printed sleeveless shirt that really showed off his biceps.

"Oh, no it's a great party," she said, "I'll come and dance soon. Why aren't you dancing?" she asked.

"Oh, I was just setting up the food table. Wanna come and help?" he asked, gesturing to the other end of the lawn.

"Sure," she said, as he pulled her off the bench. She walked with him to the long tables at the other end of the lawn.

The vibes and loud music from the dance floor made her look at the figures there, dancing to the party anthems. She saw the multicoloured lights moving on the floor and smiled to herself, thinking of her teen years. The breeze from the nearby ocean blew over the whole lawn, lending its coolness to everybody. She helped Ashwin put packets of plastic glasses on one table and making sure the food dishes were all in order. The chicken wings and the pizza smelled good, making her think of all the school parties she had been to.

"Aren't you in the mood to dance now?" Ashwin said.

"Yeah, but, not really…" Zaria said honestly. "I mean, I was just thinking…"

"Yup. Good thing some of us do that," he said, making her swat him on the arm.

She changed the topic and asked if anything was new with him. It seemed like she was seeing him after a long time though she had been in constant touch with him on e-mail. He had been seeing a girl for a few months, he had told her, but he was single at the moment. He'd finally said a firm no to the whole arranged marriage scenario his parents had been trying to get him to agree to. He stated that he had told them that he was done with meeting any more girls they wanted him to meet. The thought made Zaria feel oddly happy. That was funny, the way she was suddenly feeling so possessive of him.

Some people came over and started helping themselves to the titbits of chicken, onion rings and chips from the table. Zaria didn't feel hungry as yet and said that she would eat later.

Ashwin asked if she wanted to go for a walk on the beach.

"Just for a bit, I'm getting a little bored here," he said.

"Ok, let's go. The breeze is so lovely now," she replied.

They both walked past the pebbled patterned walkway to the gate after telling friends where they would be. They strolled down the road for a few minutes until they reached the sandy shores. The beach was mostly deserted at that time of the night except for a few quiet groups scattered around. The stars glowed in the darkening sky like a million bright lights.

The two of them walked slowly towards the sea, the fine sand sifting in their shoes. The breeze from the ocean hit Zaria's face with a sensation she loved as they stood near the sea. The sound of the waves rushing back and forth brought back all the fond memories of Chennai.

"Let's sit down for a few minutes," Ashwin said, as they were walking back up the slope of sand.

"Sure. I just love it here, by the sea," she said with a grin, plopping herself down on the sand. Ashwin sat down next to her, as she stretched her legs out in front of her and let the breeze blow her hair all over her face. The sand would ruin the back of her skirt, she knew, but she didn't mind that. She could hear the breeze wafting around her, the sound like a faint flapping but not solid, like a gush of cool, fierce nothingness. Ashwin stretched his legs out too, his black shoes pointing towards the waves that were rushing back and forth.

The smell of the salty air hit Zaria, making her close her eyes and soak in the breeze.

"Hey," Ashwin said, making her turn towards him.

"Remember when I asked you to marry me?" he said with a grin.

Leave it to him to bring up such a sensitive topic in jest. He spoke as though it was just another topic, like the weather. Zaria was caught a little off guard but smiled back at him and said, "How could I forget? What about it?"

"Well, I'd like to ask you again," he said. His tone didn't turn serious but remained jovial. "Actually I'd like to keep asking you," he continued, "But I know you'll keep giving me some reason and say no every time." He pouted exaggeratedly, with an expression like that of a dejected puppy.

"Hey, that's not true," Zaria said, surprised that her cheeks were not heating up. She saw Ashwin's expression perk up and had to giggle.

The silence was a bond between them, all the unsaid things about their feelings being spoken without words. Zaria didn't say anything else. They both just sat there and watched the waves, which lapped a short distance away from their feet. Ashwin picked up a shell from the sand and threw it over the retreating waves, which pulled it back with them.

They got to their feet and started walking back to the party. Ashwin took her hand, and Zaria let her fingers slip through his. His hand covered hers, making her feel warm and shielded. She wanted to just live for today, forget about tomorrow. When she had danced her last dance, and if Ashwin was still available why not? Life was an open book and she did want a happy ending.

Epilogue

Zaria stood by the rosewood dining table with her hands on her hips, smirking.

"Hey, if you don't turn the TV off while we eat, we will probably have a cricket divorce," she joked, giving Ashwin a playful punch on his arm.

"Wait a minute, we have only thirty runs to win or lose," he said, his eyes glued to the television set in front of him. The sound of a former Indian cricketer's commentary rang out, and had Zaria amused as usual. She heard the crowd cheer as the Indian batsman hit a boundary.

"Okay mister, but when Tara and her hubby come over this match better be over," she said, grinning at him as she sat down in the straight backed chair next to him.

The smell of the poori and chana from the hot case on the table made her reach for a spoon. She tasted a bit of the chana with onions. The spicy, tangy taste hung in her mouth as she chewed and glanced at her watch.

She was now nearly thirty-three, having hung up her ballet shoes a whole year ago, when her contract had ended. Ashwin had remained a bachelor by choice at the time, and she had married him when he had proposed to her again. They had enjoyed a honeymoon in Greece, where they enjoyed lots of intimacy in the best villas. That was all more than seven months ago, though Zaria felt like the huge wedding had only just finished the previous day.

She opened the fridge and took out a bottle of apple juice. As she took a swig from it, Ashwin came up behind her and started nuzzling her neck.

"Hey!" she protested, trying to get out of his grip as he had his arms around her. "Mister, is this the time?"

"It's just that you look really hot," he said into her ear.

She laughed. "Be careful of my stomach," she said, patting her tummy which was starting to show a baby bump.

Back in Chennai, she felt more at home than ever. She had grown to love the city even more than Moscow now, and was destined to stay in it forever. She knew India was where she belonged, having followed her heart back there. Her married life was great and she still felt like a newlywed bride. She loved her new relaxed life, without any fixed routine. She was being asked to teach ballet, and was thinking of doing it after a year or so. That would be great. Her mother and Andrei were in Moscow, sending her e-mails every month asking about her pregnancy.

Zaria was praying for a girl. Or a boy. A baby would be amazing, perfect. The start of another phase in her already eventful life.

Acknowledgements

A special thank you goes out to Lenakshmi, Fernando Aguilera and the India Fernando Ballet Company, Tatiana, Anastasia, Michelle, TM Karthik, Deepak Mudaliar and Lindsay.

I would also like to thank the following people-

My mother Anita.

Sunitha for her help in researching.

My editor Gita for her patient editing.

The whole gang of students at the Gotham writers workshop.

Thanks also to Kokila Hariram, Malini Pappan, Rajika Puri, Anusha Subramanyam, Meera, Shai, Professor Joe Hurka, Kirthi, Kelly, Samyu, Saud, Ashwini, Raksha and Sarah.